The Kindness Of Shadows

L. Chambers Wright

ISBN: 978-1-967310-35-7

Machen Society Press
11876 Stanley Valley Road
Gate City, Virginia 24251
Contact: Publisher@MachenSocietyPress.com
Website: http://MachenSocietyPress.com

Printed in the U.S.A.

Chapter 1

She despised the house. Resentment coiled within her like smoke, sharp, acrid, filling every breath until it stung to inhale. The car crawled through the soulless neighborhood, tires whispered against immaculate pavement. Each turn twisted the knife deeper.

She still refused to accept the move. The whole community was everything she loathed. The air itself seemed filtered, scrubbed clean of anything natural. It smelled faintly of wet concrete and traces of fertilizer, a chemical imitation of life. Every house gleamed too brightly, windows glinting like teeth. Grand façades of manufactured stone and glass, mausoleums pretending to be homes.

These polished places were too perfect. She kept looking for a cult sigil on every door or sentries atop towers. It was going to be an adjustment. She already had a horrible feeling in the pit of her stomach.

What she hated even more than the pompous community was Aubrey's obsession with status. It had peaked. She couldn't remember what had first drawn her to a Bainbridge. Back then, it was just another surname. He'd been just a man, sleepless, broke, exhausted from studies, with the kind of humility that she found irresistible. His hands once trembled when he told her he'd do better someday.

The change occurred over the past 10 years, but it felt like yesterday. She was still in love with him. Even if it was like *Invasion Of The Body Snatchers*. Even if she couldn't get rid of the growing apprehension in her gut. Or the image of Donald Sutherland pointing and screaming out of her brain.

Maybe the man she knew, her man, was gone. Buried beneath ambition and entitlement. A ghost she still heard sometimes, faintly, when he forgot himself. She would have stayed poor forever if it meant keeping him. Instead, she'd been left mourning a man who still stood beside her.

Now, his newest conquest was a house. "A home worthy of our status," he'd declared. The words polished, rehearsed, like he was auditioning. He hadn't asked. He'd announced. She'd been a passenger in her own life ever since.

The brick ranch they left behind, her first real home, still haunted her. The sun-warmed carpet. The uneven song of the fridge. The small, stubborn garden where nothing grew except marigolds.

It was heaven. She had dreamed of children there. Roots. Permanence. Things she'd never known in foster care. Now she was uprooted again, against her will. Her comfort traded for Aubrey's reflection in other people's eyes.

Murkwood.

Even the name sounded wrong, like something you whispered, not said aloud. It belonged in a grim story, a terrible place where lost souls wandered too far from the path. It certainly made her feel like she was in Tolkien's dark forest, under the shadow of Sauron.

A storm had gathered as they drove. The clouds overhead were bruised purple, swollen with unshed rain. Thunder rolled in the distance, low and sullen. The air inside the car thickened until it tasted metallic.

Neither of them spoke. The silence had long ago evolved from discomfort to something heavier, a third presence that rode with them. She didn't want to hear how he was now and he had no interest in hearing her at all.

They stopped abruptly after fifteen minutes of navigating one polished street after another. An immense, patinated iron gate stood between two stone pillars. *Well, at least it's different.* Maybe the house behind the gate wouldn't be like all the others. *Maybe.*

The old iron gate creaked, slow, deliberate. She half expected a guard to stop them, to check their credit score, or their

2

portfolio. Beyond, the subdivision sprawled in studied symmetry. Houses perched on manicured hills like sentinels watching intruders.

When the house finally appeared through the dense trees, her breath faltered. It wasn't the gleaming, cookie-cutter monstrosity she'd expected. No, this one had age. Character. Potential. Weathered siding mottled with gray. Stonework cracked in spiderweb lines. Muted stained-glass windows that caught what little light remained and turned it to blood and gold. It stood apart from the others, higher up the hill, inside a thick forest, as though the earth had pushed it away.

Jefferson Tate, the realtor, waited near his car, his beige suit blended with the landscape. Even before he spoke, she sensed his discomfort. The way his eyes kept darting around the house behind him.

"Ready for the keys?" he asked, smile tight, voice too light for the air around them.

She reached for them, and the metal was cold, unnaturally so. As if they had been stored in the refrigerator. The keys jingled once, sharp and out of place, before going still in her palm. Most were antique skeleton keys, while a couple of new ones indicated deadbolts on the main doors.

Tate hesitated, shifting his weight. "There's something I must disclose," he said quietly. "This property... has a reputation. A doctor lived here in the 1920s. There was—" He glanced at Aubrey. "—a scandal. Some say the place is haunted."

Her lips twitched. She almost smiled. Aubrey hated her fascination with the paranormal. Predictably, his scowl deepened. "I don't care," he said flatly. "I don't believe in luck or ghosts or any other nonsense. Hand me the pen."

Tate did. Aubrey's signature cut across the page, swift and final. She followed, though her hand felt distant from her body, as if the act belonged to someone else.

The realtor quickly left, his relief visible. The sound of his car faded down the road. It seemed to take something with it, warmth, maybe. Or safety.

Aubrey exhaled. "What a waste of time," he muttered. "Trying to scare us with fairy tales."

"It's standard disclosure," she said. Her voice came out softer than intended, like the house was listening. He didn't answer. He never did. They climbed the steps. The wood moaned beneath their feet, long, low, like a sigh.

The air changed the instant they crossed the threshold. It was colder inside. Not drafty, cold. Dust hung thick as fog, swirling around them as though stirred by something unseen.

"Aubrey," she whispered. "It feels... old."

"I remembered you liked old houses," he said. For a fleeting second, his tone gentled, and she glimpsed the man she'd once loved. "This was the first one built in this neighborhood. I thought you'd love it."

But she didn't. Not exactly. She felt something else, a pulse beneath the silence, subtle but alive. The walls seemed to hold their breath. She didn't love it, no. But she would. Somehow, she knew that.

And as she stood there, the faintest sound rose, almost too soft to catch. A creak from upstairs, or a whisper through the vents. She couldn't tell. She only knew one thing for certain.

The house was waiting for her.

Chapter 2

He orchestrated the move with surgical precision. Trucks came and went, men in matching shirts working in relentless shifts. Their movements were efficient, mechanical. She felt like a third wheel in the process. Aubrey already had everything planned before she could suggest anything.

She stayed out of the way and was eventually swallowed by towers of boxes she hadn't packed. The Bainbridge name worked like a key. Doors opened, problems dissolved, people obeyed. For once, she was grateful. She didn't have to touch the pieces of her old life as they disappeared into cardboard. It hurt less to not be there when it happened.

If you want to make someone confess, she thought, *make them pack a house.* Every object becomes a memory you didn't ask to face.

Aubrey changed the instant they arrived. She felt suspicious. The distant man of muted routines had been replaced by someone almost tender. He followed her through rooms, asked for her opinions, brushed her hand as though testing if she was still real. She didn't trust it. But she wanted to.

Sometimes his gaze lingered too long, not loving, not lustful, just watchful. The way one studies a specimen to see how it reacts. Her instincts felt alarm, but they would. Everything was new and strange. Maybe it was the house. Maybe it had awakened something dormant in him. Hope felt dangerous, but she let it flicker anyway.

The thought of a child clawed its way up again. Maybe this was it, the change she'd prayed for. A real home, a real future. His family's constant hints about heirs, his evasions, his career comes first, he's not ready, maybe all of that would finally end.

When the flurry of movers finished, Aubrey returned from the foyer. He brushed the dust from his hands. He took hers and held it gently. His touch burned with warmth. For a heartbeat, the house seemed to breathe with them, air expanding, settling.

"Are you happy here?" he asked.

His tone was soft, but his eyes probed too deeply. Something flickered behind them, something measuring. Calculating. Maybe he was struggling to return to normal. How he once was. She didn't believe it was possible at all. There was probably going to be some static from the transition. Maybe. She wasn't the girl from back then, either. They would both struggle to acclimate.

"Yes," she said, but her voice felt brittle.

He smiled, but it didn't reach his eyes. She drifted toward the kitchen. The smell of new varnish mingled with something older. A damp sweetness, like lilies left too long in water. The walls seemed to drink in her movement, the faint creak of her shoes swallowed too quickly.

Aubrey followed. She wasn't used to his attention. His presence was a pressure behind her. "How about steak tonight?" he asked. His voice light, practiced. "We'll celebrate... just us."

"That sounds perfect."

She opened drawers, touching silverware, grounding herself in the simple feel of metal. But his gaze didn't move.

"I just love to watch you," he said. The words fell heavy in the air. She wanted to believe him but couldn't. She wish all the years of negativity could be erased. Maybe she just needed time. Maybe they both did.

She froze. "Are you all right, Aubrey?"

"Why wouldn't I be?" His answer came too fast, too smooth. "You said I'd changed. Maybe I'm proving you right."

"Yes," she whispered and smiled. She still didn't believe him but didn't want him to know. Only time would tell now. He stepped closer, the air between them cooling. His hands rested on her shoulders, warm, steady, familiar, almost reverent.

"I know I've hurt you for so long," he said. "But everything I've done was for us... For you. I want to be a family again."

Again? The word caught, but before she could question it, he pulled her close. His voice softened. "This house will change everything."

She let herself sink into him. The relief was so sharp it almost hurt. Maybe he was trying. Maybe she was imagining things. He tilted her chin up. "Are you as happy as when we were first married?"

"Of course," she managed. She didn't believe what she said, either. But she would do her best to believe it. He kissed her then, deep and final, as if sealing something unseen.

"I'll go pick up dinner," he said, and with a faint smile, he was gone. The door clicked shut. The sound echoed too long. She sat on a box, heart still unsteady. *He loves me*, she thought. *He's trying.*

But then, a sound. Faint, high, fleeting. Laughter? Or just the house settling? The air shifted. The silence grew dense, textured, as though filled with invisible dust motes that moved in rhythm.

Her gaze climbed the staircase. It spiraled upward in dark mahogany, the rail polished smooth by a century of hands. Light from the stained glass above fractured across the banister, red, gold, green, colors that moved even when nothing else did.

And there, directly beneath it, another staircase that spiraled down. Descending. The air around it colder, the shadows deeper.

She should have stayed on the first floor. Instead, she climbed. Each step answered her with a groan. The second-floor hallway was dim, lined with half-open doors. The wallpaper peeled in faint curls. The air tasted of metal.

Something scraped. Slow. Deliberate. Her pulse leapt. She turned toward the sound and opened the nearest door. The room inside lay still, blanketed in dusk. Dust clung to everything. Stacked trunks, forgotten shapes under draped sheets. In the far corner, a rocking horse. It smiled at her. Paint flaked from its carved mouth, but the shape was unmistakable, too wide, too eager.

She stepped closer. The floor creaked once, then again, but the second sound didn't match her movement. The horse shifted. Just slightly. A slow, deliberate rock forward and back. Her breath stopped.

"Stop," she whispered, to herself or to it, she didn't know.

The house listened. Then the motion stilled. She shut the door with a trembling hand. She leaned against the wall. Her skin prickled, the fine hair on her arms stood tall.

Draft, she told herself. *Uneven floorboards.* But as she descended the stairs, she couldn't shake the feeling that the house now knew her name.

Chapter 3

Dinner unfolded like a portal to another time. Like the previous 10 years had never happened. She wished it was a bad dream. They laughed over tender bites of steak. Rich flavors mingled with the warmth of wine that poured as freely as their conversation. For once, she felt less like a silent housekeeper and more like the cherished wife she had once been.

He wasn't a hateful stranger anymore. He was her Aubrey. The one she married. She could burst with joy. He radiated ease. His demeanor was attentive and relaxed. It was the version of himself she thought had disappeared.

It reminded her of when they were dating. When warmth flowed effortlessly between them. By the time they climbed the stairs together, giddy with wine and laughter, a fragile hope flickered to life inside her. It cast aside the shadows that had lingered for years.

The dim bedroom greeted them like a secret. The air cool and charged with the weight of a first night in a new home. She hesitated at the threshold. A faint shiver skimmed her spine. Something about the moment felt pivotal, as if the house held its breath, waiting to reveal the shape of their future.

"We forgot to unpack the sheets," she murmured. She glanced at the half-unpacked boxes.

Aubrey grinned, a mischievous look in his eye. He pulled two comforters and a pair of pillows from a nearby crate. He tossed them onto the bare mattress with a flourish. "We'll live dangerously... sheet-free," he quipped, earning a burst of laughter from her.

They collapsed onto the makeshift bed. Their laughter spilled into the stillness of the room. For the first time in years, she allowed herself to feel safe, secure, even loved. Aubrey's warmth felt tangible, no longer an echo but something real, and she let herself believe in it, if only for the night.

The morning arrived slowly. Sunlight seeped through the curtains and cast pale rays across the ceiling. She woke first. She savored the rare luxury of watching him sleep. In the stillness, his face softened, free from the rigid expectations of being Dr. Bainbridge.

She had missed this more than she realized. The small, unspoken intimacies they once shared. She brushed her fingers lightly over the edge of the comforter. She marveled at how familiar and yet how foreign this felt.

A sharp knock broke the spell. It jolted her upright. Aubrey stirred. He groaned as he reached for his clothes. She giggled, her mood light, as they scrambled to dress.

She bounded down the grand staircase. Her footsteps echoed through the house's vast halls. In the early light, the house seemed alive. Each corner brimmed with untapped potential. Its shadows no longer foreboding but curious.

She opened the door and found three men waiting. Two stood stiff and glanced at their watches with impatience The third, a man named Bert, beamed with enthusiasm. "Mrs. Bainbridge? We're here to give an estimate on the renovations."

She hesitated but managed to smile politely. Aubrey hadn't mentioned anything about contractors. She stepped aside to let them in. She retreated to the kitchen to prepare coffee. Their voices traveled faintly through the house as they wandered. They flicked light switches and examined fixtures. The murmurs seemed to dissolve into the walls, muffled as though the house itself listened, absorbing every sound.

Bert returned as the coffee finished brewing, his cheerful demeanor unshaken. "The place is remarkable. I would estimate it's just shy of eight thousand square feet, not counting the attic or basement. When can we go over the specifics with you and your husband?"

"I'll see if he's ready," she replied. She poured steaming cups of coffee for the men. The silence struck her then, sharp and sudden. She realized Aubrey hadn't come downstairs. She thought he was getting ready when she did. It was even stranger he was home at all, but that was her own issue.

Anxiety flickered. A deep, old worry that he might retreat again. That the fragile connection between them might already be breaking. She should expect that. There were years of damage to recover from. Years of bitter loneliness.

She climbed the stairs slowly, her breath held tight as if bracing herself for disappointment. Relief washed over her when she heard the shower running. He was still here. A faint laugh slipped from her lips, and she called through the bathroom door, "Aubrey? The contractors are ready."

His voice emerged, muffled by the water. "Give me a minute. Want to join me for a quick spray?"

Her grin returned, reckless and light. She slipped into the bathroom just as he stepped out, warm droplets still clinging to his skin. He kissed her, his touch tender and lingering. "I'll meet you downstairs," he murmured as he wrapped a towel around his waist.

She lingered under the shower. She marveled at the water's pressure, so strong for an old house. It seemed impossibly pure, almost untouched, as though it rose directly from the hill's ancient depths.

The sound of Aubrey's laughter downstairs caught her by surprise. She paused in the doorway, startled by its warmth. For years, she had heard him laugh like that only with his colleagues. His humor reserved for a world she was not part of. Yet here he stood. He gestured animatedly as Bert chuckled along. Amazingly, he included her in his orbit once again.

"Gabby," Aubrey said, using a nickname she hadn't heard in years. She almost choked on her coffee. He remembered? The sound of it melted something inside her.

He gestured toward Bert. His expression brimmed with excitement. "They think we should restore the house completely, bring it back to its original design. Maybe even search the attic for old photos of what it used to look like."

She hesitated, the thought both tempting and unsettling. "Let's start with the basics," she said finally. "Strip the carpet, redo the floors, and go from there." She didn't want a house frozen in time. She wanted a home, not a museum.

The contractors nodded. Bert ordered his workers to retrieve some tools from the truck. Since the move had already happened, they decided to renovate in phases. They began pulling up the carpet and stripping peeling wallpaper. It revealed intricate woodwork and Victorian paneling beneath. *Who the hell would hide that,* she marveled. Who would use cheap paneling to try and crowbar mid-century modern out of an obvious Victorian?

She marveled at the beauty that emerged. Forgotten details whispered of another time, another life. But even as she admired it, unease rippled through her. The house seemed eager to reveal itself. She began having a strange, dark suspicion, that stripping its layers might awaken something better left undisturbed.

The shrill ring of the kitchen phone next to her shattered her reverie. She let out a soft laugh, startled by its sharpness. She wasn't used to old landline phones. They were so loud. She hadn't realized he even got the service connected. Or why. "Hello?"

"Yes, is Dr. Bainbridge there?" The voice on the other end was cold, clipped, and distinctly female.

"He's busy," she replied, irritation rising unbidden. Years of watching Aubrey prioritize calls from the lab over their life together fueled the sharpness in her tone.

"Will you give him a message?" The woman's voice remained detached, almost mechanical.

"If it's important," she said flatly.

"Tell him Dr. Andrews needs his opinion."

She frowned. "Is it an emergency?"

The woman hesitated. "No, just... no."

She hung up with a deliberate click. She didn't care for the satisfaction it brought her. For too long, they had taken him from her. It was time for him to stay.

Aubrey's voice startled her from behind. "Who was that?"

"Dr. Andrews," she said. "She wanted your opinion on something, but it wasn't urgent."

He looked away briefly. His expression flickering with something unspoken. "Did she say why?"

"No," she replied. "But I handled it."

"Good," he said softly, almost as though relieved. He disappeared into the other room with the contractors and left her alone with her thoughts.

She turned back to the window. She watched the backyard stretch under the sunlight. A swing hung from the old oak, its seat rotted, swaying faintly in the breeze. She pictured a child there, laughter filling the silence. For a moment, the image lifted her heart. It offered just a glimpse of the life she wanted so badly.

But the house felt different now. The silence wasn't empty. It pressed against her, thick and heavy, as if waiting. Voices from the other room faded, growing distant and hollow, like echoes from another time. She shook the feeling off and focused on the samples before her.

Aubrey left after lunch but said it was just to pick up some paperwork from the office. He'd taken some personal time off to get the house in order before he returned to his normal schedule. *It's nothing,* she told herself. *Aubrey would return.*

Chapter 4

He returned sooner than she expected. Less than an hour had passed since he'd left, yet he stood in the doorway again, pale and tight jawed. His breath was calming like he'd just stopped running. She nearly missed the angry red mark beneath his right eye, a fresh welt, shaped like a claw or the trace of a slap.

She reached out without thinking, her fingers grazed his cheek. The skin burned faintly beneath her touch. "What happened?"

He flinched almost imperceptibly. "Those idiots at work," he snapped. "Fully accredited scientists, and they're arguing like children over a formula." His tone was brittle, the words too sharp.

"They got physical?'

"Two did... I was separating them. I got a trophy for my efforts."

"Wow.... What formula?" she asked before she could stop herself. For years she avoided his work. It was a closed world of lab jargon and sterile ambition, but now the question left her mouth as if pulled by something else.

He hesitated. "A variety of new synthetic drugs. The main compound is *Eidophrene.* It's a hallucinogenic."

Her brow furrowed. "Hallucinogenic?"

He nodded, but his eyes drifted. Not to her, but to the dark hallway beyond her shoulder. His gaze lingered there, focused and unblinking. She turned instinctively, but the hall was empty.

When she looked back. He was watching her again. "It's experimental," he said. "It involves mostly compounds derived from phencyclidine."

The word felt strange in her mouth. "Phencyclidine?"

"PCP."

Her breath caught. "*Angel Dust?*"

"Yes," he said quickly. "But, this is controlled work, gloves, respirators, isolation chambers. No danger." But the words tumbled out too smoothly.

Her stomach knotted. "Aubrey Bainbridge... why are you working with something like that?"

He sighed, his expression tightening. "You never asked. And it's classified. Besides..." He shrugged. "You wouldn't have cared."

The dismissal stung. She looked away, her voice small. "I care now."

He touched her cheek and kissed her forehead. "Don't worry. I can take care of myself." But as he stepped past her, his reflection in the hallway mirror seemed to move half a second too slow.

The afternoon dragged, the house heavy with a silence that felt almost... expectant. She unpacked, moved boxes, wiped surfaces. Anything to drown out the growing suspicion that something was *listening.* Was it something in the house? Or was it simply the presence of her husband after years of virtual abandonment?

Shadows bled long across the floor as the light shifted. Once, out of the corner of her eye, she thought she saw movement, a figure gliding past the far end of the hallway, but when she turned, nothing was there.

By evening, the storm light returned, blue-gray and fractured. Aubrey sat across from her in the living room. His blank expression now had no trace of warmth or levity. His fingers tapped against the arm of the chair in a slow, precise rhythm, four beats, pause, four beats again. She tried to focus on the television, but her skin prickled.

"Are you okay?" she asked.

He blinked, as if waking from a dream. "Hm? Yes. Fine." His voice sounded normal, but his eyes flicked briefly toward the dark corner behind her before returning to his glass of wine. He seemed nervous.

She rose and switched on a lamp. The warm glow broke the room's spell. *It's nothing*, she told herself. *Just a house. Just nerves.*

Chapter 5

Sleep did not come easy. She drifted in and out of half-dreams, images that dissolved before she could name them. Indistinct murmurs stirred the edges of her consciousness. Voices that didn't sound quite human rasped through old walls. Shadows slid along the inside of her eyelids, never solid enough to hold but impossible to forget.

She woke once, heart racing, to the unmistakable sensation of being watched. The room was dim. The curtains breathed gently in the breeze from the cracked window.

The ceiling fan rotated slowly overhead. Its blades cut through the stillness with a soft, hypnotic whir. She turned her head and found Aubrey beside her, asleep. His chest rose and fell in an even rhythm. His skin was pale in the moonlight. The edges of his features softened to porcelain.

She reached out, touched his hand. The chill of it startled her. Cold from the sheets, or something deeper? She held her breath and then let it out in a slow stream. She tried to settle the knot in her gut.

But the unease didn't leave. It pressed in against the darkness like humidity. It clung to her skin, thickened the air. Her body felt damp and restless, as though the sheets were a net instead of a blanket.

Somewhere in the distance, beneath the house's slumber, she thought she heard whispering, soft, fragmented. Like voices echoing inside the walls. Too faint to understand, too rhythmic to dismiss.

Morning light brought no relief. Gray and flat, it poured in through the windows like spilled milk that dulled the edges of everything. She padded into the kitchen, bare feet cold on the tile. The smell of brewed coffee hadn't touched the air yet, and the house felt strangely void, still, but not empty.

That's when she saw it.

A book, lying open on the counter. The pages fanned wide, the paper tinged yellow at the corners, delicate as moth wings. The scent of old ink lifted from it dry, slightly metallic.

A medical text. She recognized the dense columns of type, the precise illustrations of anatomy, tissue, and synapse. It was one of Aubrey's med school textbooks. Something from a long-discarded box that shouldn't be on the counter.

Her eyes caught something in the margin. Her name. *Gabriella.* Scrawled faintly beside a paragraph on induced neural disruption. She froze. The ink looked fresh. Damp, almost. Her own handwriting, slanted, loopy. Unmistakable. But she hadn't written it. She hadn't even unpacked this book.

With slow, deliberate hands, she closed it. The cover thumped softly. She slid it beneath the counter. She tucked it behind a stack of kitchen towels as if hiding a loaded gun. Aubrey was still asleep upstairs. She would return it to the box whenever he left.

She moved through the house like she was trying not to disturb a sleeping animal. His presence felt foreign. It felt too large for the space, even when silent.

For ten years, he'd been absentee husband. He came home only at random. His visits were usually to pick up clean clothes, check his mail, and give her a hard time. Sometimes he would sleep at home, but usually did that in the office.

She tried to work for a couple of years, but, as if by magic, he would need so many things and have so many demands, it just wasn't worth attempting. Since she wasn't a doctor, her jobs were automatically expendable. He did it deliberately, she never knew why.

That was the past now. It wasn't healthy for her to dwell on it. He was scheduled to go back to work today. She'd expected him to rise early, bustling with mechanical efficiency. He'd vanish like always. But he lingered.

The stillness was uncanny. Not comfort. Something else. From downstairs, she listened to his alarm go off at 8:00. The tinny chime pierced the quiet like a scalpel.

She heard him move. The soft thud of feet on the floor. The low murmur of water pipes as he showered. The brush of cotton as he dressed. Familiar sounds, yet distant, like hearing a life she no longer belonged to.

He left without a word. *Now there he is.* That was the Aubrey she knew. *Well, it was good while it lasted.*

The house sighed behind him. She busied herself. Cleaning, scrubbing, polishing windows until her arms ached. She wanted the exertion, the burn of it. The smell of lemon cleaner filled the halls, sharp and bright. She tried to overwrite the scent of something older.

But by afternoon, the study was different. The air inside was thicker, stale and slightly sweet. It was undercut by something darker. Tobacco. Rich and old. The kind that lingered in leather-bound rooms and velvet drapes. The scent came in waves, like invisible fingers trailing along her skin. No one had smoked in this house.

She cautiously stepped in the study. The light filtered through the tall windows was murky, dust motes floating like spores. She didn't breathe too deeply. Slowly, she backed out, her footsteps muffled on the thick rug. She pulled the door shut with careful pressure.

Click.

The latch sounded too loud. Like a held breath released. She couldn't shake the sense that the house was changing. Somehow. it was crazy. Not just in structure, not just the scent of plaster and paint from renovation

It felt like it was *adapting.* To her. To her life. Lights she knew she had turned off flickered back on when she passed. Doors creaked open behind her after she closed them. She caught herself watching her reflection too long in the hallway mirror, expecting it to blink when she didn't.

Then came the glasses. Two of them on the kitchen counter. One she had used. She remembered the faint taste of ginger tea still clinging to the rim. But the other, clear water, half-full. Condensation clung to its sides, beads of moisture trailing down like sweat. Fresh.

Her mouth went dry. She stared at it from the threshold. Her breath felt too loud, her skin too tight. The faint purl of the refrigerator was the only sound, steady and low. And underneath it, faint as a whisper, a pulse.

Chapter 6

They renovated six rooms. The contractor said it would be better to work on one section at a time, since the house was inhabited. They concluded the renovations until Aubrey had time to inspect their work. Or until she decided what to do next. She just didn't know.

She spent the day wandering the house's endless rooms. She moved framed photos around the surfaces. She opened boxes only to close them again. She told herself she was organizing, but it felt more like pacing. Each room carried its own silence, dense, patient, as though listening. The house wasn't empty. It was *waiting*.

By noon, her unease had burrowed too deep to ignore. She slipped on her walking shoes and a sunhat, craving air, *space*. The door's latch clicked shut behind her like an exhale.

Outside, autumn greeted her with sharp, clean air that cut through the house's heaviness. Gravel crunched beneath her feet as she followed the curve of the drive. A small pond lay beneath a grove of willow trees. Their skeletal branches whispered in the faint wind.

Beyond the hedges, another house peeked through the trees, modest, sun-warmed, unthreatening. The hedge wall marked Murkwood's boundary. Nothing but normality beyond it. She missed it. She missed her old home.

Movement caught her eye. A tall, attractive man stood beside a weathered mailbox. He flipped through letters. He looked up and smiled, open, unstudied. *Normal.*

"Hello there," he called, voice easy. "You must be the new neighbor. I'm James. James Moore."

"Gabriella Bainbridge." She stepped closer, returning the smile. "Nice to finally meet someone around here."

James nodded toward her house. "Quite the place you've got. Lots of... character."

She laughed. "Feels more like I've moved into an antique store that forgot how to open."

He grinned. "Old houses do that, they hold on. My grandma used to say they keep their stories tucked inside the walls."

Her gaze drifted to her own home. Its windows bright in the noon light, glass glaring like eyes. "Stories," she murmured. "That sounds about right."

"Well," James said, shoving his hands into his pockets, "if you ever need a break from all that history, you're welcome to drop by. Working from home gets lonely, and I make a mean cup of coffee."

She smiled, touched by the casual kindness. "What kind of work do you do?"

"Programming," he said. "Mostly freelance. Boring, I know, me, the computer, and too much caffeine. But it beats an office."

"I admire that discipline," she said. "It's an isolated life sometimes."

He laughed. "You'd be surprised how much talking to yourself helps."

Their laughter mingled easily, unforced. The way she had with Aubrey before he returned to work. The tension that had sat under her ribs for days began to ease, replaced by something light, almost nostalgic, the feeling of being *seen.*

She could almost accept New Aubrey genuinely saw her, even heard her, but the years behind them made acceptance difficult. She couldn't stop feeling like an accessory that had been stored away in the closet for too long. Now that her husband decided it was time... she couldn't shake the remnants or resentment from that lonely darkness.

They talked about small things: the weather, the best bakery in town, the renovation chaos. The simplicity of it grounded her, anchored her back in something real.

Then she noticed the fog. It gathered low among the trees. Its thin tendrils curled through roots and fallen leaves. It didn't drift like normal fog. It *coiled*, slow and deliberate, as though it tested the air.

"Odd how it settles," she murmured. "Almost looks alive."

James followed her gaze. His smile thinned. "Yeah. Happens around here a lot, especially near dusk. Sometimes it gets so thick you can't see the end of the driveway."

She shivered though the day was mild. "The house feels full of history," she said. "Sometimes I swear I hear it, echoes, or whispers. Probably just my imagination."

James didn't laugh this time. His expression softened instead, thoughtful. "Old places remember," he said. "They don't always remember kindly." Their eyes met for a moment too long. Then he smiled again, bright and ordinary.

He invited her to his porch for iced tea, and she accepted. The glass clinked cool against her fingers, condensation beading down to her wrist. They talked for hours, about nothing, about everything. The ease of it was almost intoxicating. By the time 4:00 rolled around, she felt lighter, as if she'd stepped outside a dream.

"I should go," she said, glancing at her watch. "Aubrey will be home soon."

He nodded, his smile kind. "Of course. You know where to find me. Don't hesitate if you need a break from all that... character." He winked, and she laughed again, though the sound came out softer this time, tinged with something unspoken.

The walk home was quiet. Evening was coming on faster now. The sun was descending, and the mist had thickened into ribbons of gray that clung to her ankles as she walked. The air smelled faintly metallic, damp and cold.

Her house loomed ahead. A black silhouette against a dying sky. She hesitated at the porch. Dew made the boards faintly slick beneath her shoes. The upper windows caught the glint of daylight, opaque and watchful.

Something moved. A flicker of motion, quick and smooth, like someone stepped away from the glass. Her breath stilled. When she looked again, the window was empty. *Probably nothing. Just light.* Just her imagination.

She turned the handle. The door groaned open, and the familiar hush of the house met her like a held breath. Behind her, the mist crept closer to the porch. It curled along the threshold, stopping just shy of the step, as though waiting for permission to enter. She shut the door and leaned against it, listening.

The silence felt thick again. But this time, beneath it, she could swear she heard the faintest sound, not quite a whisper, not quite a sigh. Something like a voice saying her name.

Chapter 7

The house gleamed with a strange vitality. Two weeks of renovations had peeled back decades of dust and rot. She hadn't thought of a proper name for the place, so it would just be *Murkwood* until then. The word no longer represented oppressive rows of identical houses. Now, it was just home. The one house that didn't look the same.

Murkwood breathed again. Its polished floors shone with an almost human warmth, and its tall windows caught the light like open eyes. She sat on the Queen Anne sofa. Her fingertips glided absently across the velvet. The muted afternoon sun streamed through the glass, pale and filtered. It cast narrow gold slashes across the room.

Above her, the restored ceiling fresco had painted cherubs and angels in soft pastel clouds, delicate, serene. But their eyes. Their eyes never stopped watching. She told herself it was only the angle of the light. She told herself that every time.

Knocking sounds had started appearing randomly. Sometimes it sounded like someone was knocking on the front door. Sometimes the back door. Sometimes the knocks were in the floor or the ceiling, or on an interior door. She'd chalked most of it up to the disturbance they'd caused in the house. New building materials. New flooring in several rooms. It was bound to cause some new quirks and would probably settle once the renovations were completed.

The phone rang and disturbed her thoughts. The sharp, shrill tone shattered the stillness like glass. She jumped. Her hand clutched at her chest before she reached for the receiver.

"Hello?"

"Gabriella?" The voice was familiar, cool, crisp. *Francis Bainbridge.*

"Hello, Francis," she said, trying to sound bright. "Aubrey's at work."

"Oh." A pause, soft but hollow. "Tell him I called."

Then the line went dead. The silence that followed felt different, not just empty, but *weighted.* As though the echo of Francis's voice had been absorbed by the walls and was now spreading through the house molecule by molecule.

Francis had always been unpredictable, charm one minute, frost the next. Something about the call unsettled her. The brevity. The lack of... exit.

She carried Aubrey's coffee cup to the kitchen. The faint scent of him, cedar and espresso, clung to the rim. Through the window, the swing beneath the old oak moved gently back and forth, though the air was still. The frayed ropes creaked softly. The seat tilted, caught mid-motion, as though pushed by a small, unseen hand.

She stared.

A vision flickered behind her eyes: a child laughing, legs kicking high, auburn curls flying. Her heart tightened with an ache both sweet and unbearable. Then...a sound. A slow, scraping rhythm from above, followed by a drag that vibrated faintly through the walls.

The hair on her arms lifted. It came from the third floor. For days she had heard things, faint giggles, running footsteps, and convinced herself it was children from the neighborhood together with the home's strange acoustics. But this sound was heavier. Intentional.

Someone wanted her to hear. She climbed. Each step creaked like a warning. The air thickened as she ascended, turning humid, resistant. By the second landing, her breath came short. By the third, it felt as if the air itself pressed against her, slow and deliberate.

The scraping stopped. A faint rustle followed, behind the door at the end of the hall. It was one of those that hadn't been renovated. She was still deciding what to do with the extra rooms. Her hand trembled as she reached for the porcelain knob.

It was cold, slick, as though someone anxious had just released it.

She turned it. The door swung open. Dust hung in the air like smoke. Pale light bled through the curtains and pooled over the trunks lined along the wall. And then she saw him.

A man now stood at the center of the oddly vacant room. There were no boxes, no clutter from former occupants any longer. He was tall and still, dressed in a black. His high-collared suit belonged to another century. His skin had the dull sheen of wax, and his posture was exact, deliberate.

For a moment she thought he might speak, but his mouth never moved. Only his eyes did. They were the color of voids, black without reflection, without depth. They fixed on her, and something inside her went silent.

"Get out!" she said. The words quivered out of her. "Or I'll call the police!"

He didn't flinch. He took a single defiant step toward her. The sound of his shoes, or what should have been sound, never came. His movements were utterly silent, yet the air around him *shifted*, as if the house itself recoiled.

The temperature dropped. Her breath clouded in front of her. He was close now, close enough for her to see the faint impression of veins under his skin, black, not blue. Then, behind him... two pairs of feet protruded from under a sheet on the bed.

Pale. Motionless. There were two bodies. Dead. The toes of both were frozen in unnatural configurations. Their skin was mottled and waxy. The world tilted. A strangled cry caught in her throat.

His lips curved into a smile slowly, mechanically. It was like he knew she noticed the bodies. They revealed teeth too white, too pointed. A smile too wide but never reached his eyes. He raised a hand, elegant, gloved, and touched the doorframe beside her.

She pressed herself against the wall and slowly backed out into the corridor. Her pulse thundered. She couldn't move further. Then, with a sudden jerk, he *slammed* the door shut.

The sound cracked through the house like a gunshot. Footsteps finally sounded. They retreated, soft, steady back into the room, until they dissolved into nothing. She stood frozen. Her heart hammered against her ribs. Minutes passed before she dared move.

When she finally forced the door open, the room was empty of the earlier changes. He was gone, as were the bodies. The silent trunks had returned. The bed was stripped bare. The air reeked faintly of iron and decay. Only one thing had changed. The wallpaper had peeled away near the baseboard, revealing a streak of color beneath, robin's egg blue.

It pulsed faintly in the light, as though freshly painted.

Her fingers shook as she pulled more paper away, the edges curling under her touch. The color spread beneath, luminous, impossibly clean. It felt... *alive.* She couldn't tell if the stain were paint or burned into the plaster.

One of the trunks stood slightly ajar in the far corner. She opened it. The hinges groaned like a sigh. Inside were brittle photographs, families staring stiffly at the camera, their faces drained of warmth. Beneath them lay a newspaper clipping, folded and yellowed.

Model City News, February 16, 1920

Dr. Reyland Hayes learned yesterday that his beloved wife was gone. Authorities have given up the search and declared her dead. Dr. Hayes reported that his wife, Alura, had taken their son's death too hard. She grew sick afterward and never recovered. She disappeared from her bed during the night. Dr. Hayes has our deepest sympathies.

Her breath shuddered. The words reached across time, threading into her like a chill. She almost heard them. The mother's voice, soft and desperate, the child's laughter dissolving into nothing. And beneath it all, something else.

A man's whisper. Low. Coaxing. As if someone very near her ear was saying, *"Welcome home."*

Chapter 8

The morning felt hollow. She woke to a silence that didn't feel empty but *expectant*. The air itself seemed to listen. Aubrey's absence left the house lighter, yet heavier somehow, as though it mourned his leaving, or worse, *approved.*

Eight weeks into the new house and his hours were slowly going back to normal. Apparently, that honeymoon was over. His mood was also regressing. She could see threads of the old hateful Aubrey again. He now came home around 8:00 in the evening. He frequently left before she woke. If he came home at all.

It didn't bother her as much as she thought it would. Maybe it was just too late to rekindle that flame. Her afternoons consisted of checking the mail and chatting with James. It was nice to have a friend. She wasn't as isolated as she feared in the midst of the communal sterility.

She rose determined. Today would be different. Today would belong to her. As she showered, her palm pressed gently against her stomach. The water ran warm, the air fogged thick, and for a moment, hope took shape inside her, fragile, luminous, fleeting.

Then the phone rang. It woke her from her dreams. Its shrill tone ripped through the house like a blade. "Hello?"

"Gabriella?" Francis's voice, brittle but familiar.

"Francis?" Her heartbeat quickened. Her mother-in-law rarely called without purpose. "Is everything alright?"

Francis didn't answer at once. The silence on the line hummed faintly, static wrapping her words. "There's something I need to show you. Something I haven't shown anyone... But it must be confidential."

Unease slid down Gabriella's spine. "What are you talking about?"

"Has Aubrey been home all week?"

The question hit oddly sharp. "Yes. Of course. Why?"

"Well, on second thought... you should come here," Francis said. Her voice shifted, low, urgent, commanding. "There's a package. I can't explain it over the phone. Just... come before four."

"What's in it?"

A pause. Then a sigh, fragile and frayed. "Something you should see. Its urgent." The line went dead.

She stood still. The receiver pressed to her ear long after the dial tone began. She filled her insulated tumbler with water from the new dispenser. She didn't know why Aubrey got a water cooler, but it was good water. She was always fine with the filtered water from the refrigerator.

She didn't want to go, but she had to. She always believed Francis never liked her, but she had never known her to lie. If she said it was urgent, it probably was. The butterflies in her stomach were massive. Every mile made them larger.

The Bainbridge estate loomed from the mist like a temple to Mammon. Sprawling gardens, marble fountains, windows that glittered coldly in the gray light. Francis waited at the entrance. Her frame was narrow and severe in a slate dress. She wore single pearl brooch at her throat. Her expression was unreadable, until Gabriella noticed the tremor in her hands.

That was strange by itself. No butler. No maid. It had to be really bad. She got out of the car. "Follow me," Francis said as she briskly turned. They quickly walked back into the house.

"It looks so empty," she didn't like the silence. She was already anxious.

"The staff has the evening off."

Inside the glass-walled lanai, the world muted. All color and sound muffled by old money and restraint. It was kind of nice to be there without staff approving or disproving and fussing over her.

Francis poured bourbon with shaking fingers. The liquid sloshed against the rim. "Sit."

She obeyed.

"I've debated getting involved for a long time..." Francis stared into her drink as though the truth swam there. "But I think you deserve to know. I only recently had proof."

She drew out a thick brown envelope from beneath the cushion beside her. She placed it on the table between them. Her touch was hesitant, reverent, as though she handled something necessary but toxic.

She wasn't sure it she should open it or burn it. She finished her drink. She tore the package open and turned it up. The contents spilled out: receipts, letters, invoices. A disorderly confession. She picked one up, a hotel bill. Another, a jewelry receipt. The next, a handwritten note in Aubrey's looping signature. Her breath faltered. "What is this?" she asked softly.

Francis's smile was small and bitter. "What do you think?"

She looked across the papers, each heavier than the last. Gifts. Dinners. Hotel suites. His name on every line. "An affair." The word felt foreign on her tongue.

It didn't shock her as much as she imagined it would. It actually made sense. Their life together the past 10 years was inherently dysfunctional. But weren't all families dysfunctional? She just hadn't counted on this level of dysfunction.

"Of course," Francis said simply. "Did you think you'd be the exception? Bainbridge men don't love women, they *collect* them. Until the novelty fades. Then, they put us away and forget about us."

She shook her head, disbelief clinging like static. "Why tell me this?"

Francis drained her bourbon and set the glass down with a hard clink. "Because you have a chance."

Her voice softened then, unexpectedly tender. "I didn't. By the time I learned what your father-in-law was, I was too entangled, six children, a name I couldn't escape. You still can.

For some reason, Aubrey hasn't saddled you with children. I don't know why but take advantage of it. Get out while you can. I'll help you, if you need it."

"Why help me?'

"I hoped for Aubrey to be different. That maybe he took more after me. It started so well. Aubrey was so wonderful when you were married."

"I know."

"I had no idea, until recently, what your marriage was like. I can't watch someone go through that. Why didn't you tell me?"

"Aubrey said no one in his family liked me."

"I wonder why." she mused as she stared at her ice. "That's never been true."

"I didn't think he'd lie..." she admitted. "I've never had a family, so I'm ignorant of the finer details. I thought maybe that's just how families were." She ruffled through the documents. Everything pointed to Dr. Leigh Andrews. She had the nerve to call their home.

The weight of her words settled between them. Francis refilled their drink. Her eyes shone faintly. "Jacob was charming. Brilliant. Everyone adored him. But the lies were constant, and seamless. I thought I'd married a man; I married a *mask*."

Her hands trembled around the empty glass. "I told myself Aubrey would be different. But Bainbridge men... they inherit their secrets like blood."

Her voice cracked. "Why didn't you tell me this was a potential problem *before* we married?"

Francis's gaze snapped back. "Would you have listened?"

The question landed like a slap. She said nothing. No, she wouldn't have believed it. She would've thought his family was just trying to break them up. She didn't know how to respond to Francis. She was clearly distraught as well.

They sat in silence. Rain pattered faintly against the glass walls. She sat back and listened a moment. She wished she'd been closer with her mother-in-law.

Francis continued. "There's another name.... *Dr. Andrews.*"

Gabriella's pulse jumped. "Dr. Andrews? I know her."

"She calls often," Francis nodded. "Always emergencies. Always private. I thought she was a colleague. Until I wasn't sure."

Gabriella's mind flashed to the phone call. *Dr. Andrews needs your opinion.* The chill that crept over her then returned now, deeper.

Francis leaned closer. Her eyes softened with something like pity. "You see now why I called you. I've already spoke with my attorney. He will help you... If you like."

She rose slowly. It was going too fast. She couldn't keep up. She just learned about Aubrey's secret life. She tried to leave graciously. She needed air. She needed to move.

Her voice barely audible. "I... I need to go. Thank you for this... for everything." She scrambled to get all the papers back in the envelope.

Francis caught her wrist. Her grip was surprisingly strong. "You're not alone," she whispered. "If you need me... call. No matter what happens."

The drive home blurred. The sky had turned the color of steel; the trees leaned toward the road like witnesses. Francis's words circled in her mind. *Bainbridge men have secrets.*

Aubrey's warmth. His gentleness. The new attentiveness. It all seemed like a bad performance now. The charm of a man who knew fate had already caught him and needed her to stay. Maybe that was why his attention felt so strange. it wasn't just a matter of being accustomed to affection. It was false affection. It was all a lie.

When the house came into view, its shape loomed darker than before. The windows reflected no light. She should hate the house. After all, it was what Aubrey wanted, not her. But she didn't hate it. She couldn't. It was starting to feel like home. Her home. His absences just reenforced the sense that is was hers.

Inside, the air was electric, the stillness oppressive. The house was aware something happened and was waiting for her reaction. She was waiting for her reaction, too.

She just couldn't react. She felt numb. She could be crushed. She could be devastated. She just wasn't. Her relationship consisted of microscopic breadcrumbs. Sweet moments so minuscule and so impossibly rare that she questioned their very existence.

The mirrors along the hall shimmered faintly as she passed. Her reflection warped at the edges. Her eyes looked a fraction too late to follow her own movement.

Then, a sound. A child's laugh. Soft. Distant. Echoing up from the floor beneath her. She froze. The laughter came again, lilting, playful, threaded with something else. Something sharp.

Outside, the swing moved in the windless dusk. Its ropes creaked in slow rhythm. The air thickened with the scent of wet wood and old roses. Francis's words echoed in her mind. *They have secrets, Gabriella.*

She felt like the envelope was dirty, or something to be ashamed of. It was ridiculous. It was just stuff. Every time she touched it, she kept waiting for Aubrey to walk in. But, even if he did, would he care? Probably not. She hoped.

She decided to keep it in the study. She'd started the study for Aubrey, but when it became clear he was just going back to his old habits, she took it over. She enjoyed researching on her own sometimes. Particularly in areas of the paranormal or other fringe sciences. Aubrey hated it. True crime was another area of interest but never got the reaction she liked.

She flipped through the papers. So, Dr. Andrew's was the *other woman*. It was pathetic. She didn't know if she should hate her or pity her. Aubrey adored her when the lab hired her. She was a Harvard educated scientist. She was going to bring such *prestige* to the company but turned out to just bring that prestige to his bed. She didn't hit a glass ceiling so much as a glass mattress.

Maybe she needed to ascertain when the affair began. That would probably be relevant moving forward. It was clear it was no regrettable moment or passing fascination. It had gone on for at least two years.

Why did Francis amass this dossier? Or get someone else to compile it? Mothers didn't keep such things on their sons, even wealthy ones. She knew that much. The documents went back several years, so had she hired a private investigator? Who else could've gathered them?

She dropped the information into the desk drawer. Her mind still couldn't move past Andrews. For all her education, all the discipline she had to possess, she was nothing more than a *homewrecker.* A mundane, common, ordinary, run-of-the-mill homewrecker. That had to be a blow to her ego.

She would expect it from a honkytonk barfly. From a clubbing raver, maybe. Never an ivy-league educated scientist. It was amusing. Did the mistresses of Bainbridge men have to hold pedigrees? But it was also so sad. The woman with an impeccable resume came in second place to someone that had a real estate degree, but no license.

Aubrey was the villain in their story, however. He wrecked the lives of two women, instead of just one. Well, two that she knew of. There could be many, many more women as evidence came forth.

She backed away from the window. In the reflection of the glass, behind her trembling outline, she thought she saw movement, a child's small figure darting past the hall. When she turned, the hallway was empty. Only the house remained, awake now, remembering. And this time, she agreed with James. It did not seem to remember kindly.

Chapter 9

The silence between them was thick, not absence, but pressure. It filled the air like fog. She was now thankful for it. She didn't know what to say. The horrible Aubrey had returned in full force.

She'd hidden the folder. He didn't even suspect she knew about his second life She would examine it more after he left. She needed to contact Francis's attorney. Aubrey hadn't touched her in weeks. Again. It was for the best.

She'd considered having an affair, but it was so messy. She wasn't interested in bringing an innocent bystander into their dysfunction. She could always get a one-nighter, but that seemed equally pointless.

Aubrey sat slumped in the armchair. The posture of a man unspooled. Something weighed on his mind. His shoulders, once squared with habitual pride, had folded inward. His face was pale, drawn tight with exhaustion and something else, shame, maybe, or fear he refused to name.

She sat opposite him, hands clasped tightly in her lap. She pretended to watch television. She had started a paranormal programming marathon before he came home. He was quiet now. No remarks. No snide comments. She kept waiting for the inevitable guffawing or eyerolling, but it didn't come. The quiet wasn't companionable; it was alive, sentient, heavy enough to make her bones ache.

A cold draft coiled through the room. Damp. Deliberate. It brushed her cheek like breath. The papers on the floor rustled, stirred by air that didn't belong. He was oblivious. She had a gut feeling that whatever was in the house didn't exactly like her but liked him even less.

Then came the sound, a low hiss, soft and human. A sound shaped like a word that refused to form. Her skin prickled. She wanted to speak, to reach out, to bridge the widening gulf between them. It was just too late. But the house spoke first.

A *creak*. Above them. Slow. Heavy. Another. Not the scatter of expanding wood or the casual moan of an old structure. These were footsteps. Rhythmic. Pacing. Her heart thudded. The sound was directly above them, as if someone were walking the length of the room in careful, deliberate strides.

She looked to Aubrey. His eyes had snapped open, sharp with awareness. He didn't want her to know he was startled.

"Aubrey," she whispered. "Do you hear that?"

He nodded slowly. The fear in his gaze mirrored her own. The footsteps stopped. The sudden quiet was worse than the sound. "Probably just the wind."

For a moment, even the air felt still. Then a soft vibration moved through the floorboards, so faint it could have been imagination, except she *felt* it, a pulse beneath her feet.

"It's just the house settling." Aubrey said at last. His voice was too even. The calm of a man pretending not to crack.

Something in the room shifted. The air thickened. It pressed against her chest. The walls... breathed. Not outward, not visibly, but the pressure changed, like inhalation and exhalation drawn through plaster.

Then came the laugh. High. Thin. A child's laugh. It floated down from the stairwell, bright and wrong. Laughter without warmth, amusement without joy. Aubrey stiffened, his hand gripping the chair. His lips parted, but no sound came.

"Did you...." He couldn't finish.

She nodded. She'd heard that laughter before in this house, faint echoes, fleeting. But this was *close*. Personal. It wasn't playful; it was *mocking*. It rose again, nearer this time, weaving through the hallway like a thread.

"Probably the wind," she said weakly. She knew how absurd it sounded.

"I'll check," Aubrey muttered, already on his feet. His movement broke the spell, but it didn't ease her fear. It deepened it.

He crossed the room. His footsteps loud on the floorboards, defiant against the encroaching quiet. She wanted to stop him, but the words stuck in her throat. Then she remembered the envelope. The lies. The treachery.

As he reached the staircase, the overhead light flickered, once, twice, then went out. Darkness swallowed the house. For a heartbeat, she still saw him, a silhouette cut from shadow. And behind him, movement. A darker shade within the dark, standing too close, too still. She blinked. It was gone. The light returned.

"Aubrey?" She trailed behind him.

He didn't answer. His hand gripped the banister, white-knuckled. Then he began to climb. Each creak of the steps echoed like a heartbeat in her ears. Halfway up, laughter returned, softer now. It curled through the dark like smoke. It coiled around his name, around *her*, until she couldn't tell if she was hearing it with her ears or somewhere deeper.

He looked back once, his face ghost-pale in the thin light. His eyes found hers, wide, terrified. And then the whisper came. *"Liar."* It hissed through the room like steam escaping from a wound.

Her stomach turned. What was that about? The word hung there, not loud, but *true*. Aubrey froze mid-step. His hand tightened on the banister. "Gabriella," he breathed. "Did you hear that?"

She nodded, unable to speak. The single word pulsed between them. It echoed off the walls like judgment. She was afraid to speak. She almost told him it was because he was.

Suddenly, it felt dangerous. As if holding that package or even knowing about that life was a threat to her own. Or to Francis. But what could possibly be *threatening* about it? That seemed melodramatic. She didn't know why her gut even went there. Worst case scenario would be divorce. Unpleasant, yes. Threatening? No.

The sound of footsteps started again, heavy this time. They paced from room to room above their heads. Each one deliberate. Each one closer.

She clutched her arms. The cold seeped deeper into her bones. "Aubrey," she whispered, "it's an old house settling. Let's go back downstairs." She didn't feel like chasing ghosts with him. Besides, *only morons, dolts, and dullards believed in that sort of thing*, as he said so many, many times. When she never asked. Maybe she didn't want him in her world either.

But he didn't move. He stood at the top of the stairs; eyes locked on the landing above. His body was rigid, caught in invisible threads. The air pressing, pulsing, *listening*. For a moment, it sounded like he was whispering, but not to her.

Then came the stillness. A silence so absolute it roared in her ears. She took a trembling step backward. The house seemed to lean closer, watching, waiting. They weren't studying it like it was studying them

Something flickered at the edge of her vision. A movement above, human in shape but wrong in its attempt. Then it was gone. Only the hush remained.

The faint laughter stopped, but its echo clung to her. It curled around her shoulders like cold hands. And she knew, truly knew, that whatever lived here wasn't haunting them. It was *judging* them, as if trying to decide who to target first. And it wasn't finished.

Chapter 10

As October sank into colder days, she felt the shift not only in the air but in her bones. The wind that once carried the scent of rain and soil now bit with a sharper edge. It whispered through the trees like a voice she almost recognized.

Not much had changed. She had an appointment with Francis's attorney, but it was going to be two weeks before she could get in for the initial consultation. There didn't seem to be any better way to fight a Bainbridge than with one of their own attorneys.

Aubrey still puzzled her. For a brief and miraculous window, had been present, attentive even, as though the house itself had revived something dormant in him. But that fragile reprieve had crumbled. Now, the distance between them was as vast as ever.

The pattern was the same as before. Just like ten years earlier, he started to come home a little later as time passed. He offered soft apologies and half-smiles that didn't reach his eyes.

"The lab's been busy," he murmured.

She was crushed back then. His absence destroyed her. It was so much like a death. She struggled with depression for years after the change. She got through it. The person she loved was gone. He would never be back.

She was given a brief reprieve when they moved. She knew it. She had one last glimpse of the person she fell in love with. She didn't know why it felt so final this time.

It was for the best. They no longer had anything worth fighting for. He now shrugged off his coat with mechanical grace, with mechanical excuses. But as the days bled together, his absences lengthened. The air grew colder, the nights darker, and Aubrey faded like a figure stepping backward into shadow.

Within a couple of weeks, his returns were transactional. A man refueling between worlds. He ate without tasting, spoke without meaning, moved without presence. One evening, they sat across from each other in the low amber light of the dining room. The silence between them became unbearable. The tick of the antique clock sounded like a heartbeat that no longer belonged to either of them. Her fork hovered over her plate. Her courage gathered like breath before a storm.

She opened her mouth to speak, to ask why he even came home, but the shrill ring of his phone cut through the stillness. Without hesitation, Aubrey rose. His voice, low and muffled, drifted from the next room, clipped phrases, professional, distant.

Ten minutes later, he returned, already slipping into his coat. "I have to head back to the lab," he said. His tone was flat, almost rehearsed.

She stared at the untouched food between them. "Now?" she asked quietly.

He didn't answer. She didn't expect him to but figured she would go through the motions. The front door closed with a hollow echo that reverberated through the house. "Oh, no, not that," she sarcastically spoke to herself. Her flat emotionless voice surprised even her. "Whatever will I do?"

For a long time, she sat alone at the table. Her hand clenched around her fork. The house absorbed the silence. Its walls expanded around her grief, like lungs taking a long, satisfied breath. In his absence, the house came alive.

She'd cried so hard, for so long back then, she'd just ran dry. That was years earlier. It was sad, but she was done. He could be someone else's problem now.

The quiet pressed into every corner until it no longer felt empty but *aware*. Doors she knew she had shut stood ajar by morning. Footsteps moved through the halls at night, soft but deliberate. They paced above until dawn.

Then came the whispers. Faint, formless, but near. Sometimes she thought they were words, half-heard syllables that slipped through the edges of sleep. Other times they were breaths. They brushed her ear like a feather.

One night, passing the staircase, she froze. A figure stood at the top, feminine, motionless. Her head was bowed as though she was mourning. The air around her shimmered faintly, the dark fabric of her shape blurring into shadow.

Her pulse eased. The figure's sorrow was palpable, almost tangible. It spilled into the air like perfume. Then, in the blink of an eye, she was gone. The staircase stood empty. But the grief she left behind clung to the banister, to the air, to her skin.

By morning, the house felt heavier. Even the light seemed dimmer, diluted through curtains that hung limp as shrouds. Her chest ached with the need to breathe something real, something untouched by the house's weight.

She grabbed her coat and stepped outside. The brisk air hit her like ice water, sharp, cleansing, almost shocking. The air smelled of rain and wet leaves, of something honest. The breeze clawed through her sweater, but she welcomed it.

The world beyond Murkwood felt fragile and alive. Distant birdsong and the crunch of gravel beneath her grounded her to the earth. Her home was beautiful in the morning air. Mist swept around her and everything she encountered.

As she neared the edge of the property, she spotted James in his garden. He crouched beside a row of ripened squash. His flannel shirt was rolled at the sleeves. His hands worked through the soil with practiced ease. A wheelbarrow sat nearby, filled with potatoes and a few ripe pumpkins.

He glanced up and smiled. The kind of smile that acknowledged her, not as a ghost in someone else's story, but as a person. "Gabriella," he said warmly. "Out for a walk?"

She tried to smile in return, but it wavered, fragile as glass. What was happening to her? For a moment, it felt like she had no control. He stood and brushed the dirt from his palms. "You okay?"

Her lips parted, but no words came. The effort of pretended steadiness felt too heavy today. She cleared her throat and tried to force a smile. "I think so."

He read her silence. "You look like you haven't been sleeping."

"I guess I haven't," she admitted softly. "but I'm sure it's just anxiety from the move. It was sudden. Aubrey's... gone most nights now. I thought moving here would change things... but it's the same."

James's expression darkened. "Still working those late hours?"

"I don't even know if he's working." The admission spilled out before she could stop it. "I want to believe he is, but I can't... shake this feeling. Like something's wrong. Like he's...." She stopped. The words felt dangerous. "like he's somewhere else."

He hesitated. He then stepped closer. His voice low and careful. "I take it things have gotten worse?"

"Yes, I hoped they wouldn't but figured it was coming."

"I'm sorry."

"You don't have to be sorry." She shouldn't be telling him this. She quickly added, "Really, I'm used to it... An old pro."

"Does he really work that much?"

"I doubt it."

He leaned closer and whispered. "Do you think he's seeing someone?"

The question hurt more for its gentleness. She didn't answer. Her silence was enough. His hand brushed her shoulder, a simple and human gesture. "I'm sorry," he said. "You deserve more than that."

Her throat tightened. The world felt small for a moment, quiet except for the wind threading through the trees. She wasn't accustomed to genuine sympathy. Or any genuine emotion, for that matter.

His voice softened. "It must be hard, being alone in that big house. Especially when it doesn't feel... friendly."

She exhaled. The truth escaped with her breath. "It's not that bad, although sometimes doesn't feel friendly. I keep hearing things. Footsteps, whispers. And once..." Her voice faltered. "I saw someone. A woman. At the top of the stairs."

His gaze sharpened, though his expression remained composed. "Do you know who she was?"

She shook her head. "No. She just... watched me. Like she was grieving. But it wasn't just sadness, it was like she *recognized* me."

He was quiet for a moment. His eyes flicked toward her house beyond the trees. "Old places remember," he said finally. "Some remember more than they should."

His words hung between them, heavy, honest. For the first time in weeks, she felt a real human connection. "Thank you," she whispered. "For listening."

He smiled, not pitying, but warm, grounding. "You're not alone, Gabriella. If anything happens, or if you just need to escape those walls, you know where to find me."

The walk back felt longer. She could've talked to him much longer, but she didn't want to be a burden. The last thing she wanted to give her only friend was toxic venting. If she recounted all her hardships, he would miss planting season in the spring.

The air had turned brittle by the time she started back. The sun was sinking low. It painted the world in bronze. When she reached the house, the weight of it returned, its tall frame dark against the sky, its windows blank and unblinking.

She paused at the threshold. Her hand hovered over the doorknob. For a moment, she swore she saw movement behind the living room curtains, a flicker, a shadow, but when she blinked, it was gone.

Inside, the silence folded around her like a waiting embrace. She shut the door softly and stood in the foyer. Her breath fogged faintly in the cold air. The house exhaled, a long, slow sigh, as if satisfied she'd returned.

And then she heard it. Somewhere above, faint but unmistakable, a whisper. It coiled through the air like smoke, brushing her ear as it passed. One word, stretched thin and longing: **"Stay...."**

Chapter 11

She laid awake in the stillness of midnight. Her eyes traced the shadows that swayed across the ceiling. Skeletal branches clawed restlessly at the windows.

The cold pressed against her, familiar but no less suffocating. She kept fearing the front door was open, but it never was. The walls murmured faintly, their groans and sighs too synchronized to be random.

Sleep had abandoned her days ago. She was always prone to bouts of insomnia but excessively so now. Nights stretched on endlessly. Filled with half-heard whispering memories of warmth that had long since drained from the bed beside her. Aubrey's absence cut sharper at night. The empty space where he should have been throbbed like an open wound. The silence grew teeth.

She closed her eyes and tried to steady her breathing, in, out, in again. But even the rhythm of her own body felt out of sync with the house's slow, natural rhythm.

Then she heard footsteps. Soft, deliberate. They moved just beyond her door. Her eyes snapped open. Her pulse thundered in her ears. *It had to be the house settling. It had to be.* But the steps didn't fade. They advanced, each one slow, measured, as though whoever, *whatever*, walked wanted her to listen.

Her instinct screamed at her to stay still. To pull the covers over her head. To pretend sleep. But some deeper, more dangerous impulse stirred. The pull was almost *inviting*. She rose.

The floorboards were cold beneath her bare feet. She slipped her robe over her shoulders and opened the door. The hallway yawned before her, dark and endless.

The air was damp, with a faint metallic tang that clung to the back of her throat. The old wallpaper in the hall, faded roses and ivy, seemed to ripple at the edges of her vision. The patterns seemed to shift if she didn't look directly at them.

The sound came again, ahead of her now, just beyond the guest room. She hesitated. Her hand hovered above the glass knob. *Go back*, her mind whispered. But her hand didn't listen.

The knob turned easily. The door creaked open. The room waited in stillness. Everything was as she'd left it. The old iron bed, the lace curtains, the mirror propped against the far wall. Yet the air was dense, cloying, sweet with rot.

A smell, floral and metallic, like lilacs masking something dead. Her stomach twisted. She stepped inside. The floorboards shifted beneath her weight, their groans low and wet, as if something beneath the floor moved with her.

Then she saw it. An old floor-length oval dressing mirror. Its cloudy surface glimmered faintly in the dark, like water disturbed by an unseen hand. Her reflection was there, pale, drawn, her eyes too wide, but behind her, the darkness deepened.

And within that darkness, a figure. Faint at first. Then clearer. It stood still, shape wavering, like smoke rising in reverse. Human, but hollow. She froze. Her body betrayed her. Her reflection didn't move, but the figure behind her leaned closer.

She shuddered. The air grew colder, the scent sharper. Then...nothing. The image flickered and vanished. It left only her haunted eyes staring back A sound escaped her, small, helpless, and she stumbled back. Her hand flew to her mouth.

The room seemed to tilt. The air buzzed faintly, a vibration just below hearing. She didn't know if it was her or the house. She was exhausted.

She fled. The door slammed behind her. The hallway stretched before her, impossibly long. Four doors became eight, then sixteen. The faster she ran, the longer the hall grew. Instead of sixteen doors, there were thirty-two.

Shadows deepened into something alive. They writhed and danced on the walls. The walls hummed and then moaned. Eventually, they roared.

By the time she reached her bedroom, her legs trembled, her lungs tight as though she'd run a marathon. She collapsed onto the bed, her body rigid. The silence settled around her.

She heard the faint tremble of something. Something rattled on the dresser. She looked over and found her three Armani porcelain ladies now watched her. For a moment, it felt like they glared at her. She pushed them back where they were supposed to be.

Her attention drifted toward the window. Outside, the swing beneath the old oak moved in slow rhythm, though the night was perfectly still. A pale glow emanated from it, faint and unnatural. It illuminated the ropes as they strained under invisible weight. The creak reached her ears, long, deliberate, almost mournful.

"It's just the wind," she whispered, but even as she said it, the air in the room pressed colder. The swing continued its steady arc. Each motion was deliberate, like it tried to recall how it should move.

She turned and buried her face in her hands. She could feel a headache coming on. Her mind split between reason and something older, deeper, whispering the truth: *The house isn't haunted... it's alive.*

She returned to bed. Hours passed. Sometime before dawn, exhaustion pulled her into a shallow, uneasy sleep. That's when she felt it. A weight, gentle, but undeniable, sank into the mattress beside her.

The faintest dip, as though someone had just sat down. She froze; breath caught in her throat. Then came the touch, cool fingers brushing her cheek, tender as a lover's, deliberate as a test. The hand was so small and cold.

She almost returned to sleep but remembered she wasn't in her brick ranch and no one else was there. Her eyes flew open. She turned. The bed was empty. Pale morning light filtered through the curtains. It painted her room in soft tones. But the indentation remained. A faint hollow pressed into the blanket. The space where someone had been.

Chapter 12

Downstairs, the house was quiet, but it was a different kind of quiet now. Aubrey's coffee mug was in the sink. It was strange. The only proof she had of another living soul in the house were the remnants of what he used. She couldn't help but feel that it included her. Like Francis. They were accessories to be stored away and only acknowledged on special occasions.

Aubrey left the coffee pot on. *And I thought there was nothing left in my marriage,* she thought sarcastically. Her hand trembled. The mundane act felt absurd in this world that no longer obeyed reason. He must've just come home for clean clothes.

She turned toward the window. Her eyes were drawn unwillingly to the swing. It hung still. For a moment, relief flickered through her, until she saw it.

A child, standing beneath the tree. A small figure, half-concealed by the mist. Barefoot. Still. Its face was pale and unreadable, its eyes dark and depthless, not cruel, but *ancient.* The child looked directly at her. She blinked, and it was gone. Only fog. Only air. But the impression lingered, that gaze, that terrible knowing.

She whispered to herself, "It's just my imagination." The words sounded absurd, hollow, wrong in her own voice. Because deep down, she knew she hadn't imagined it. The walls seemed to push against her. The air buzzed with invisible energy.

Suddenly, it was four in the afternoon. She couldn't understand it. Had she stared out the window for three hours? Impossible. She looked down. A half- empty glass of water sat beside the sink. It was fresh. She didn't remember getting it or drinking it. Condensation dripped down the side.

She needed to see someone... *anyone.* She was just tired, that was all. Tired and lonely. She needed fresh air and maybe to see a friend. She grabbed her coat and went out to walk the fence around her property. The air helped her clear her mind. When she reached James's yard, he looked up from his work, his expression softening with concern.

"Gabriella," he said. "You look..." He hesitated. "Like you've seen a ghost."

Her laugh came out broken. "Maybe I have."

He straightened. He brushed the dirt from his hands. "You're shaking. What happened?"

She wanted to tell him everything, the mirror, the footsteps, the swing, the missing time but the words tangled in her throat. Finally, she managed, "James, do you ever feel like your house is... watching you?"

He frowned slightly, thoughtful rather than dismissive. "Old houses have memories," he said. "Sometimes they remember wrong. You'll get used to it. It's natural with old houses."

She swallowed hard. "This one remembers too much."

He studied her for a long moment. Then, gently, "Do you want to come inside? You don't have to go back right now."

The offer was kind, and for a moment, she almost accepted. But something deep within her resisted, as though the house itself had hooked its fingers into her spine. She didn't know how much she should involve him. He was right next door. What if it were something that could migrate to him?

"No," she said softly. "I can't. It wouldn't... like that."

He blinked. "It?"

She forced a weak smile. "Sorry, brain freeze. I mean Aubrey wouldn't... Just a feeling." She had no idea how Aubrey would feel, but blaming a house wasn't a good way to keep a friend. The last thing she needed was to be the neighborhood kook, or for Aubrey to hear she was spreading rumors of a haunting. She would never hear the end of his mockery.

His voice softened. "You're not alone, Gabriella. If you need me..."

"I know," she said quickly. "Thank you." She smiled and turned before he could say more. The walk back felt longer than ever. it didn't help that she felt more alone than ever. The world was so big, and she was just a mote of dust.

The house loomed ahead. The late light caught in the windows. It made them glow faintly, not with reflection, but from within. When she reached the door, her hand trembled as she turned the handle. The air that met her was cold, sharp, and wet.

She heard people talking. *"Please, Reyland..."* A woman begged.

"Go back to your clinic room."

" I don't belong there."

"Of course you do"

"No, I do not."

"It's the fever talking Allura."

"No, it isn't,"

"You either rest or you can go to the asylum."

"You wouldn't."

"Of course I would. Be grateful I'm doing what I am. You don't deserve more. Charlie died because he had your weakness."

Those voices belonged to living breathing people. There was nothing ghostly or subtle about them. She considered calling 9-1-1 first, but they would probably run when she found them. She needed a description of what they looked like. She burst through the kitchen door.

Only the kitchen was empty. Her porcelain teapot had been moved from the display cabinet. It now sat on the table with two matching cups. They appeared empty, but warm, like they still held tea. Her house was just weird.

She knew they were properly put away when she left. She *knew* it. There was no question. But there they sat, right in front of her. Maybe the house was haunted. Or she was crazy. Or both.

She needed to distract herself. She wondered who Aubrey was seeing. Was it just Andrews, or did he have a litany of affairs? Maybe there was something wrong with her. Maybe she wasn't crushed because she wasn't sane enough or something. Maybe he'd driven her crazy years earlier and she was just lucky to be as functional as she was.

She never believed Aubrey would do something so "middle class" as so many average situations he pretended to be so far above. But he was now middle class. He was now one of the very "plebeians" he ridiculed. Oh no, he would never *stoop* to adultery. How dare she think something so common about him?

He was a trophy wife and sports car away from perfect mediocrity. She chuckled to herself. James was right. Talking to yourself did help.

She went inside the living room. The door shut behind her with a soft click. And then, from the stairs above, faint, like a breath carried through distance, came the whisper again. This time, clearer.

"Stay... stay... stay."

It wasn't a plea. It was a command.

Chapter 13

The late evening shadows draped the Bainbridge estate in a darkness that seemed to move. The day was as cold and blustery as she felt. The attorney congratulated her on having so much documentation. That envelope Francis gave her contained most of what they needed. Anything else would be a bonus.

Francis asked her to come by afterward. She was secretive again. She wasn't as shocked to see another package had been delivered. She was incredibly grateful to someone. She just wished she knew who was behind it. Aubrey had dedicated coworkers. They ran the department at the Bainbridge Institute, and from what she'd been able to gather over the years, it was ran like high school.

She admonished their cruelty if she heard him talk about it. One of the first issues to put a wedge between them was his behavior at work. She didn't appreciate his assholery, and he didn't appreciate her normality. He became cock of the rock, far from the sweet, humble, and genuine man she married. Maybe that man never existed, to begin with.

The box sat beside her in the passenger seat, plain, brown. It pulsed with a kind of silent menace. Another strange present from an even stranger source.

Even without touching it, she felt it thrum like whatever was inside was alive. She gripped the steering wheel tighter. Her knuckles white against the dim glow of the dashboard. She didn't want more material. The shit would hit the fan as it was. As much as she liked the idea of an end to the drama, she knew she'd have to earn it. Aubrey wouldn't make anything like that easy. Nor would he be decent.

This time, the package was addressed specifically to her, but in care of Francis. It also had a horrible handwritten note.

Her mind replayed the note again and again. *He's playing with fire. This is beyond you. Get out before it's too late.*

The handwriting was jagged, urgent, almost violent. She could still see the indentations pressed deep into the paper, as though whoever wrote it had carved their warning straight into the fibers.

Each word carried a pulse of its own. Each word felt true. Francis opened the package to see what was inside but didn't want to know the extent of it. She made that clear. She couldn't blame her. Aubrey was her son and would always be her son. Nothing he did actually reflected on Francis, but it was apparent she felt it did.

She risked a glance at the box again. The papers within, chemical formulas, notes, fragments of something colder than science, seemed to murmur beneath. Words *psychological hazard* and *hallucinatory risk* had burned into her mind, looping endlessly like a chant.

Who sent it? And why to Francis's house, not hers? Did the person know to trust Francis? Maybe Francis was really the one behind it all to help her leave, done anonymously, to avoid any backlash from the family.

She hadn't been out at night in longer than she could recall. She stopped to get a pizza on her way home. The one thing she could count on was freedom. He didn't care what she did. That was the only redeeming quality of her marriage. As long as none of his peers or family found out about it, she was fairly free. The only exception was travel. Her place was at home, another of his favorite pearls of wisdom. She needed to compile all his lectures in a book. *Pearls of Wisdom for Assholes.*

His work habits started innocently enough. A few extra hours here and there. A research convention one weekend a year or so. It was perfect. She was happier than she ever imagined possible. Somehow, it all slipped away. Before she knew it, he was hardly ever home. It was a gradual process over a couple of years, but it seemed so fast.

His hours drew out longer and longer. His schedule got to her for the first few years. She eventually grew resentful and broke things to get his attention. It did at first. She tired of it before he did.

She drained $200,000 from his account and transferred it to a private account of her own. She believed that would get his attention more than anything. She imagined he would be furious, that he would demand she return the money instantly.

In retrospect, it was irresponsible and petty, but it made no difference. He didn't care. Maybe he never knew about it. She still had the money and regularly added cash to it. She didn't know why but it seemed wise.

When she first did it, she didn't think he would go through the complications of divorce, but she didn't trust him. His Bainbridge lawyers could put her out in a heartbeat, and she wouldn't have anything.

After he ignored the drain on his account, she knew then their relationship had ceased to be what it was before. She hated obsessing over their marriage. It was pointless. It was ridiculous. But she woke up one day and her marriage was her world.

She loved the house but wished he hadn't pretended to be the old Aubrey. It brought back so many things she'd repressed. She liked it repressed. She liked the mechanical coldness she could depend on. Why did he pretend he was human again? It was doubly cruel to lose him twice.

Outside, the moon hung low, a pale eye peering through the ragged clouds. When she pulled into the drive, the house loomed in its glow. Its silhouette vast and silent. The oak in the yard swayed faintly though the night was still, and beneath it, the swing moved, slow, deliberate, back and forth.

Her headlights caught a figure. Small. Still. Watching. A boy. Her breath caught in her throat. The shape flickered, the shadows bending as though reluctant to let it go. She blinked, and the figure was gone. The swing continued its steady, empty motion. *A trick of the light,* she told herself. *Exhaustion. Nothing more.*

But as she stepped out of the car, the air wrapped around her, damp and charged. The scent of roses reached her nose, faint and sweet and rotting. She barely kept her balance with the pizza and the new mystery box.

Inside, the silence waited. It greeted her the moment the door closed. It swallowed the faint noises of the outside world. The house was so still it felt suspended, every sound swallowed before it could form.

She set the box on the dining table. Her hands trembled. No. There was no rush She would eat and relax first. She grabbed an icy soda and streamed an episode of the *X-Files* in the living room. Aubrey hated that show.

She ate and put the task off for two episodes. She still didn't want to look through the box 's contents. It was just going to be more betrayal, but someone wanted her to see. Someone went to a lot of trouble to get it to her. She at least owed it to them.

She took the box into the study. She decorated the renovated room with a dark academia theme. Aubrey wouldn't use it, but she liked it. She turned all the lamps on and placed the box on the antique oak desk.

She opened the lid and lifted one of the papers. The words wavered, the ink seeming to shift beneath her gaze, the formulas swimming out of alignment like disturbed reflections in water. She blinked hard. The words steadied again, stark and clear.

Phase P: patient displays cognitive delusion induced by prolonged exposure.

Subjective reports: apparition-like distortions, perceptual bleed-through, synthetic empathy responses.

Her pulse quickened. What was this? What had Aubrey been doing? What on earth did any of this have to do with her marriage troubles? It was a cheating spouse, not industrial espionage.

She thought of his drawn face. The mark on his cheek. The way his eyes darted to shadows when he thought she wasn't looking. Maybe this wasn't ordinary research. It wasn't medical advancement. It was tampering, with the mind, maybe with reality itself.

Suddenly, the move didn't seem so random. Maybe there was another reason. Could the house be a part of his research, and not just a "status symbol." She didn't know how it might be related to his research but that didn't mean much. She couldn't understand why or how, but for some reason, she suspected the house was tangled in it.

Her thoughts slipped back to the boy. That solemn figure she'd seen again and again. His gaze wasn't haunting; it was pleading. She felt it now, as surely as her own heartbeat. He needed her. Maybe she needed him, too.

She reached down under the stack of papers. She felt photographs. She brought several up to examine. They looked like surveillance photographs. Aubrey stood with a woman in a hotel lobby. His arms were around her. They looked happy.

The second photo was of Aubrey in the lab. The hotel woman stood beside him, and they examined something on the computer.

She returned the items to the box and closed it back up. She was too damned tired to deal with it. She would catalog and examine everything tomorrow. Hal Deskins, Francis's attorney, didn't think there was reason to rush the proceedings.

She climbed the stairs. The house sighed faintly around her. The air grew thicker as she ascended. She didn't have to worry much. On the unlikely event he actually came home, he would go to bed first. They'd been there for months, and he hadn't even inspected what the contractors had done to the house.

The hall stretched long and narrow. Its light was dim and unsteady. The wallpaper's faded flowers seemed to twitch in the corners of her eyes. It pulsed faintly with color that wasn't really there.

She stopped at the guest room door. It was open just a crack. Something faintly tapped inside, soft, deliberate, rhythmic. Like fingers drumming lightly on glass. Her pulse jumped. She reached for the knob and pushed the door open.

The room lay steeped in shadow. The mirror stood where it always had, tall and tarnished, its surface hazed over like a window fogged with breath.

The air smelled wrong, a strange blend of metal, lilacs, and something sharp. Sort of like ammonia, but different. She took a step forward. The boards moaned beneath her feet, a slow, drawn-out sound that made her skin crawl.

Then the mirror shifted. Not a trick of light. Not her imagination. It rippled, the reflection darkening as though something beneath the surface had stirred. And then she saw him.

The boy.

His face was pale, his eyes wide, too wide. His small hand pressed against the glass, his mouth moving silently before a voice, faint and far away, reached her.

"Need help..." The sound was thin, like air passing through a crack in the world.

Her throat closed. "Who are you?" she whispered. "What do you want?"

His lips trembled. His eyes flicked past her, toward something behind her. She turned, heart hammering. Nothing. Just the dark. When she faced the mirror again, the boy's expression had changed. Desperation sharpened into fear.

"Need help..." The voice was louder now, fractured. It echoed in the walls, in her chest, as if the house itself repeated it. The air grew thin. The temperature dropped sharply. Shadows uncoiled from the corners of the room. They stretched, twisted, warped, the shapes almost, but not quite, human. The scent of flowers grew overpowering, sickly sweet.

She stumbled back as the mirror rippled violently. For a single, horrifying instant, there was *something else* behind the boy. A darker figure, massive and formless. Its eyes glowed like embers. The boy's face twisted in terror.

Spiderwebs of frost raced across the mirror's surface just before it outward with a sharp crack. She looked away as the shards passed. She fled. Down the hall, down the stairs, into the living room where she collapsed on the sofa.

She clutched the throw to her chest as though it might anchor her to something real. Her body trembled. Her skin felt bruised with cold. The boy's voice echoed in her mind, faint but insistent. *"Need help..."*

Over and over, until it became part of her breathing. She buried her face in her hands. Her tears hot against her palms. Whatever haunted this house was no longer content to stay hidden. It wanted her attention.

A haunted house was the *last* thing she needed. She already had enough to contend with. Her marriage was over. Her closest friend was her mother-in-law, who she had an equally troubled relationship with. James was a good friend, but she couldn't pull him in to all that trauma.

Equally strange was the bizarre sense that she belonged in the home. No matter how much horror the house unleashed, or what terror it held, it was her place. The house had claimed her, at some point, and she claimed it. Now, they were intertwined. She wanted the house. Period. it was her house. Aubrey could have everything else. She just wanted a home.

She eventually fell asleep on the couch. Aubrey didn't come home at all. *Screw him.* She felt like she had a hangover, but she didn't drink the night before. Maybe she was coming down with something.

The dawn came gray and muted. The house still and hollow around her. But she felt something stir. She couldn't explain it. It was almost like a vibration beneath the floorboards. The faint breath of something stirring just out of sight.

She couldn't distinguish if it were real, or just her. She could be developing a flu. She felt her forehead to see if she had a fever. She didn't.

She rose and looked toward the stairs. Her reflection caught briefly in the windowpane. For a heartbeat, she saw movement. A small hand pressed against the inside of the glass.

The landline phone beside the sofa rang. She jumped up and grabbed it. "Hello?"

It was Aubrey. "Aubrey?" She certainty wasn't expecting him to call. Maybe she was still dreaming.

"Are you awake?" his voice was oddly normal. He never called unless he was angry about something

"I am now." She chuckled. There had to be a punchline somewhere.

"I had to ask you something."

"What?"

"Have you seen father?"

"What?"

"Father. Have you seen him?"

"Your father died before we met." Now it was getting weird.

"No, no, no. *Father*."

"You make no sense."

"Father has seen you… he likes you."

"Oh, really?' she was getting tired of his riddles. "Where did he see me?"

"The guest room." The line went dead. She would've been scared if it wasn't so damned strange. Who the hell was father? Why would she care if the liked her? There wasn't anyone in the house to be father. The contractors finished their work until she decided the next project.

Aubrey didn't call her. Ever. Let alone on the landline. He probably didn't even knew her number unless it was programmed. He wouldn't go to the trouble of actually dialing numbers for her. He certainly didn't have sense of humor enough to prank her. She checked the caller ID, but it only read "unknown."

She waited for him to call back and clarify what he was talking about, but he didn't. She texted him and asked if the called, but he wouldn't answer until later. He never did.

Then nothing.

Only the house… waiting. She slowly began to realize the house might be sending her a message. Maybe the boy wasn't just asking for help. Maybe he was *warning* her.

Chapter 14

The tension in her chest grew heavier with every passing breath as she moved inside her home. The door closed behind her with a sound too loud in the silence.

It was another day. Thanksgiving approached and she felt bitter. She usually did around the holidays. She always wanted a family to celebrate with. A husband and children, who would gather around the table. She still didn't have one. Every season she hoped it would be the last the was alone.

Francis used to have a large Christmas dinner for the family, but all of Aubrey's siblings moved away. She always felt like an outsider there, but at least she wasn't alone. It didn't do any good to dwell. She needed to distract herself. Usually, she liked to paint or research something interesting.

This year, however, she had unwanted topics to research. She knew she had to. People got divorces all the time. Some were messy. Some were simple. There was something unusual about her situation. She didn't know why, but it felt like it was going to get much worse. The anonymous packages offered proof of that. Her gut still hadn't eased when thoughts of that entered her mind.

The house seemed darker than usual, steeped in its own stillness. Every corner sharp and waiting, as if aware of what she carried. Waiting to catch her. Or waiting to see if she was caught.

She retreated to the study to puzzle over the mysterious box. She pulled it from under the desk and shook its contents out. Most of the papers showed signs of wear. Their curled edges no longer cut. The folds were losing their crispness. Someone had kept them for a while before she got them. The dates ranged back as far as 3 years.

The scrawled warning burned in her mind. It was etched there as deeply as the words had been pressed into the paper:

He's playing with fire. This is beyond you. Get out before it's too late.

She'd looked over many of the pages, but she still only scratched the surface. Many were still marked "**confidential**". Most were "**sensitive data - do not distribute!**" There were even documents marked "**for official use only.**" some had official seals that looked much like military insignia. Was it even legal to have them?

Several pages discussed human trials for some substance called, Eidophrene. She had never heard of it. It sounded ominous. Considering what he admitted to working with before, she couldn't imagine what other chemicals he didn't mention.

She unfolded one of the pages with shaking fingers. The handwriting inside was tighter, neater, colder. Each line of data felt clinical, detached, but the meaning pulsed with quiet horror.

NEURAL DESTABILIZATION.
ADVERSE COGNITIVE SHIFTS.
HALLUCINATORY ANOMALIES.

The words crawled across the paper like insects and burrowed under her skin. Outside, the last smear of daylight bled away. The kitchen dimmed until only the faint hum of the refrigerator kept her tethered to the world. Then came the chill, slow, creeping, deliberate. It wasn't the kind of cold that slipped in from a draft. It seemed almost sentient.

She turned toward the window. The latch was fastened. No air should have been moving. Yet something in the room exhaled, soft, invisible, but alive. Cold.

The pages fluttered in front of her. Her heart jumped. One of the folded sheets came open on its own. The corners lifted as though they were turned by unseen fingers. The script stared up at her, black and glistening in the faint light:

EXCESSIVE EXPOSURE TO COMPOUND E7H9 LINKED TO DESTABILIZED STATES OF REALITY. SYMPTOMS INCLUDE AUDITORY AND VISUAL PHENOMENA.

Her pulse thudded in her ears. *Wait.* Why did it unfold this paper? Was this what she'd been experiencing? The footsteps, the laughter, the boy? Were they symptoms, or something else altogether? The strange flu symptoms that came and went?

It seemed like she would know if she were ingesting a chemical. The only meds she ever took were an occasional Tylenol or antacid. He was never around when she cooked or made a drink to spike those.

Her hands trembled as she folded the papers. She tried to shove them back into the box. The rustle of paper sounded too loud, too alive. The more she touched them, the more she felt as though she were handling something *contaminated.*

She needed a break. She'd spooked herself. Aubrey was capable of many things, but she couldn't see him risking his career like that. Not to experiment on her. Besides, he could lose everything he held dear. He didn't love her, but he adored his work. He would never jeopardize something he protected so religiously.

There were a handful of miscellaneous photographs in these papers. One, apparently Aubrey's desk, was included. He still had the mad scientist mug she'd gotten him when he first started research work.

Then... something else. Her heart dropped. She ran and got a magnifying glass.

It couldn't be.

It just couldn't

There was a *family* photograph on his disk. He was with the same woman from the hotel lobby. With three children. *Three fucking children.*

She ran to the bathroom and threw up. What the hell? She waited for years just hoping for a child. She even went through a phase of wanting to adopt. Aubrey wasn't going to stay home long enough to conceive anything, not even an idea.

She placed the opened papers in the folder made. She closed the box back up and locked everything in the desk's bottom drawer. She carried the key on a small key fob attached to her phone. She wished Aubrey had just punched her instead.

That's when she felt it, that familiar shift in the air. Not a sound. Not yet. Just presence. Someone was behind her. She froze. The hair on the back of her neck prickled as the silence deepened, not empty but *watching. Waiting.* It felt like they were standing on top of her.

Then came the sound. *Tap.* A faint, deliberate tap, not from behind her, but from the study. Then another. *Tap.* The rhythm was steady. Slow. Expectant.

She walked toward the doorway and stopped. The space beyond was black. The edges of furniture barely visible in the gloom. Something shifted there, faint, subtle, like the air bending around a shape. And then she saw him.

The boy.

He stood in the far corner, half-consumed by shadow. His eyes impossibly dark and deep. His face was too still, too knowing.

Her breath broke. "What do you want?" she whispered.

He didn't speak. Instead, he lifted his hand and pointed toward the desk. The temperature dropped instantly. Her lungs burned with the cold. The air smelled faintly of iron and rosewater.

He took a step forward. His lips parted. His voice, when it came, was thin and distant, like a whisper trapped between dimensions. "Help...."

The word cut through the air like a blade. Her back hit the threshold. The box shifted inside the desk. It sounded like it would rattle out the side before it fell over. Papers whispered inside as though restless to escape. The boy's gaze flickered with sorrow, with pleading, and behind it, something like terror.

Before she could move, a deep, resonant *thud* shook the ceiling above her. She flinched, her head jerking upward. Another thud. Then another. Heavy footsteps paced directly above her. Slow, measured, as if something slow and enormous crossed the upper floor. They were in the master bedroom, from the sound of it.

The boy was now gone. The air collapsed inward. The cold retreated all at once and left a vacuum in its wake. She spun, searched the shadows, but the room was empty. Only the echo of those footsteps remained, and even they faded into silence. She returned to the locked drawer and opened it.

The box flaps had come undone when it fell on its side. The contents had spilled out. A paper inside rustled faintly, though there was no breeze. That was the final crack in her composure. She grabbed her coat. She clutched a few papers and fled. Maybe she should keep it all hidden, but she felt like she was going mad. She just couldn't overlook the family photo on his desk. That should be her. Those should be her babies.

The night air hit her cold, merciless, clean. It felt *real* in a way the house no longer did. She sat in her car for a while and considered her options. Where could she go? She didn't want to go back to the Bainbridge estate. She trusted Francis but not the staff. She certainly didn't want to put her in a position to examine those documents any more than she had.

She barely remembered the drive to James's house, only a blur of headlights, the tightness in her chest, and the whisper of that warning looping in her mind: *Get out before it's too late.*

She was startled to find James already at the door when she pulled into his drive. Concern was written across his face. She wasn't expecting him to be awake. She wasn't really expecting him to even answer the door.

"Gabriella?" he said. He stepped out onto the porch. "It's nearly midnight. What—"

"I'm so sorry to disturb you. I need to show you something." she cut in. Her voice didn't sound like her own. "I need a fresh perspective. I don't know what's happening in my house... Or to me. I need to tell someone. I'm so sorry you're the only person I have to tell."

He led her inside. His home warm and softly lit. The air here didn't make any noise. The shadows didn't move. She sank into his couch and clutched the box like a lifeline.

"It's okay." He seemed startled by her apologies and her earnestness. "Really. It is okay. Just unexpected."

There was no graceful way to do it. There was no genteel manner to throw open her marriage or its decay. She laid the papers out across his coffee table. Words, diagrams, notations, all written in Aubrey's unmistakable hand.

She caught her breath and calmed herself while he walked to the table. He leaned over and scanned them quickly. His brow furrowed deeper with every line.

"Jesus," he muttered. "What does he work in? I haven't seen materials like these since the lab in college. I think this is... a controlled compound study. I think. But this..." he tapped one of the pages, "this is neurochemical instability. They're describing symptoms like psychosis, paranoia, hallucinations."

Her throat was dry. "It was sent to Francis, Aubrey's mother, anonymously. The note said I need to get out before it's too late."

He looked up sharply. "Do you think Aubrey's using this on people? Experimenting?"

"I don't know." Her voice cracked. "But the boy, he keeps coming back. He keeps asking for help."

James's gaze softened, but fear lingered in his eyes. "Then whatever Aubrey's mixed himself up in... doesn't seem to just be chemistry anymore."

She swallowed hard. "What do you mean?"

He hesitated. "He's working with some serious clients, and on a wicked substance. Opening doors he won't be able to close. Some doors, once you open them, don't close. Science... the human mind... it is all the same, Gabriella. Once you start tearing at the veil, something may come through."

The words sank into her, slow and heavy. The papers lay between them, pale and silent. She didn't know what else to say. He offered his guest room, but she declined. She needed to get it all locked away. She didn't trust anything related to it. Some of those papers were copies of obviously classified documents.

Would the military descend on her for holding sensitive information? She was relatively sure most were copies, but that probably wouldn't matter. The point was she had them. She didn't want anyone near with that kind of risk.

She left with, "I'm sorry again to bring this in your life. I don't have any family. I didn't know if I should involve the cops. I have an attorney but won't see him again for another week." She stared down at the box. Her pulse loud in her ears.

"It's fine. Stop apologizing." He smiled. "I think we're in similar situations. My family lives across the country. I moved here with an ex years ago. She grew up here and had all the friends. I swore I was going to move back. I just never did. Truthfully, I like helping. I seldom get to talk to anyone."

Their conversation faded into comfortable silence. She was glad she came here. It was embarrassing, but at least she was humiliated in front of a friend. Her heart hurt worse than anything.

The boy's face flickered in her mind again. She didn't have real children, Maybe she could at least adopt him. She heard his voice. *Help.* The sound echoed through her memory, faint and desperate. And in the distance, beyond the safety of

James's walls, the Bainbridge house waited. Murkwood. Alive. Aware. Listening.

Chapter 15

The night pressed in close. It clung to her like wool. Every creak and sigh of the old house rang too loud, as if the building had huddled over her to listen. The walls seemed to pulse faintly in rhythm with her breath. It was like an organism that wrapped around her and exhaled whenever she did.

Maybe she should've stayed with James. It just seemed wiser to return home and to bring her trauma with her. Besides, if she was really starting divorce proceedings, she didn't want Aubrey's lawyers to learn she'd spent the night in another man's house. For any reason.

She returned the box to the desk and changed into her pajamas. She drifted barefoot through the hall. The wood beneath her toes was cold and rough, each uneven grain scraped against her skin like a warning carved into the floor. The shadows didn't seem to be simple darkness; they had mass. They leaned toward her when she passed.

A soft rustle came from above. Then the long, slow protest of the attic floorboards. She froze. The banister under her hand felt slick. It seemed to expand and contract beneath her touch as if breathing. No second sound followed, but the feeling remained: something unseen hovering just outside of reach.

She went to the kitchen. The air there was no warmer. A smell caught her, damp soil, mildew, and the papery scent of old pages gone to rot. It lingered like a memory that wasn't her own. The refrigerator hummed, the wall clock ticked, both too loud in the hush.

She filled the kettle, the metal lid clattering like a gunshot in the quiet. She needed tea. A cup of chamomile should help her relax.

It's just fatigue, she told herself. *Just nerves.* She clung to the lie until her cell rang. The unexpected sound split the silence and she jumped. It was almost two in the morning. Who on earth would call?

The display read "*Unknown.*" Her hand hovered over the accept button. Dread closed her throat. Still, she picked up.

"Hello?" she whispered.

At first there was nothing. Then, a hush, thick and charged, like the air before lightning breaks. The hair on her arm prickled up. From inside that silence, two voices began to surface, warped, distant, yet unmistakable.

"*...once this project is done, we'll have everything we've been working toward,*" said a man's voice. Affectionate. She knew that tone, even though she hadn't heard it in ages. *Aubrey.* Even through the distortion she knew him. The careful cadence. The confidence that always sounded like arrogance. Her stomach turned to stone.

Another voice answered. A woman's, low, playful, intimate. "*I can't wait. We'll finally be free of all the secrets. Our family will be whole.*" The words slithered into her ear like poison. *Free of all the secrets.* Her grip on the phone tightened until her fingers ached.

"*Did you decide what to do about Gabriella?*" the woman asked, amusement curling through the question.

Aubrey laughed. A warm, practiced sound she hadn't heard in years. Even when they first moved in and he seemed to be returning to normal, he hadn't laughed like that.

"*She's wrapped up in that ridiculous house. Let her play while we handle the work. The place is already working its magic...she's practically unraveling herself. We'll get her out of the way in no time.*"

"*How effective has eidophrene worked?*"

"*It's been magical. She's convinced the house is **haunted**.*" They softly laughed together.

"*She should like that.*"

"*Don't remind me.*"

73

"What about the neighbor?"

"Oblivious. Hopefully he'll be a good witness when she really loses it."

The line went dead. *She's practically unraveling herself....*

The phone slipped from her hand and hit the counter with a hollow crack. The sound seemed to echo forever. Her knees threatened to give way.

She caught the edge of the counter to steady herself. The world around her pulsed in and out of focus. *She's practically unraveling herself....*

She would not have believed it if she hadn't heard it herself. It was so impossible... so unbelievable. Was *she* the experiment*?* Was that the real goal behind the move? Aubrey. And another woman. Laughing. *He'll be a good witness when she really loses it*

Her chest constricted until each breath came in short, trembling gasps. The words replayed like a recording she couldn't shut off. *She's practically unraveling herself.*

She couldn't wrap her head around it. Would he risk it all to experiment on her? *Her?* Nonsense. No. It couldn't be possible. It was impossible. She felt sick again.

Something brushed the wall behind her, fabric against plaster, faint but real. She turned sharply. The boy stood at the end of the hall, small and still. His face illuminated by a shaft of moonlight.

His eyes, dark and solemn, locked onto hers. No menace. Only sorrow... deep and old, the kind of grief a child should never know. Slowly he lifted a hand and pointed first at her, then toward the front door.

"What is it?" she breathed. "What are you trying to tell me?" He didn't answer. His form flickered like a candle drowning in wax, and vanished.

Her heart pounded so hard she thought it might break her ribs. She looked to the door, the one he pointed at. She saw through the sidelights of the front door. The porch light spilled across the yard in uneven patches. The trees shifting in the windless dark. She hesitated, then reached for the lock.

Beyond the porch, the yard stretched into blackness. For a moment she saw nothing. then something *moved.* A figure stood at the edge of the property. Tall. Motionless. Cloaked in the dark. It watched her.

She stumbled back, slamming the door shut. The bolt clicked home with a shuddering finality. She pressed her back to the wood, the cold seeping through her clothes. The hallway behind her was empty now, but the weight of the boy's gaze lingered. It echoed in the hollow of the house. The structure groaned, shifting slightly, as if sinking deeper into the earth.

She slid down the door and sat there. Her breath came in ragged pulls. The kettle whistled in the kitchen, a lonely, distant wail. When she finally forced herself to stand and turn it off. The silence that followed was worse, a thick, quiet.

She drank the tea, but it didn't help. Hours later, dawn crept pale and weak through the curtains. She hadn't moved from the couch. The house seemed to hold its own breath, patient and alive, as though it understood something she didn't yet know. Whatever it wanted, it wasn't finished. Her husband wasn't either.

Chapter 16

Tension had simmered for days before it finally boiled over. She sat at the dining room table. Her eyes remained fixed on the plate before her. His untouched food had long gone cold. She thought he would at least have supper with her. Nope.

Upstairs, his footsteps retreated, steady, deliberate, until they faded into the hush of the hall. He just came home to get his clean clothes and drop off his soiled clothing. Even the sound of him walking felt like a wound. The silence that followed was thick and electric.

Her fists clenched against the table. The air itself seemed to vibrate with restraint. She couldn't keep ignoring it. Not after what she knew. Not after all the evidence. The chair screeched against the floor as she rose. That single, jarring sound sliced through the quiet like a blade. She crossed the foyer and began her climb.

She wasn't going to breathe a word about what she had. Not the envelope. Not the cache of documents. Not even what she heard when his phone butt dialed her. She could talk about the generalities. She didn't have to provide details.

Each step up the staircase felt like wading through molasses. The air grew colder and denser. Shadows seemed to shifted unnaturally before they pooled in the corners. The faint golden glow of a bedside lamp spilled into the hallway ahead, guiding her toward the confrontation she'd avoided for too long.

Aubrey stood by the window when she reached the room. His back was turned. His posture was straight, rigid, a man who pretended to be content.

The moonlight caught the edge of his profile when he turned slightly. It highlighted the fatigue carved into his face. He was getting ready to put on fresh clothes, so evidently he wasn't going to stay. He still wore his rumpled shirt as he loosened his old tie. The perfect picture of a man halfway between guilt and pretense. He tried to straighten his appearance. "Is something wrong, Gabriella?" His tone was sharp. Controlled.

"Yes," she said. "Something's very wrong."

The faintest smirk tugged at his lips. "Well, by all means... enlighten me. What now?"

"Don't," she snapped. The words came out before she could stop them. "Don't talk to me like that. Don't be a smartass. I know, Aubrey. I know about *Leigh.*" The name cracked through the air like glass breaking.

For a fraction of a second, his expression faltered. Guilt flickered, quick, unmistakable, before it vanished behind practiced indifference. He turned away, fingers grazing the cold windowpane.

"Francis has been talking to you," he said quietly. Not a denial. Not even surprise.

Her voice wavered. "You're not even going to deny it? And why do you think it's Francis? You know we don't speak." She lied, but she wanted to protect her only ally. "You are surrounded by people every day. You really think your attitude inspires loyalty?"

He sighed, as though exhausted by her very presence. "It doesn't matter. What would be the point? You've already made up your mind."

The words hit harder than she expected. A hollow space opened in her chest, grief bleeding into fury. "Made up my mind? Do you even care?" she demanded. "Do you even feel *anything* about what you've done?"

Aubrey's eyes found hers, cool and steady. "Gabriella," he said evenly, "this is exactly why I didn't want to have this conversation. You've always been so—" he paused, choosing the word carefully, "—*emotional.*"

She let out a bitter laugh, the sound harsh in the still room. No. No more eggshells. No more being who she was back then. "Gaslighting doesn't become you.... *darling.* Don't make this about me," she said. "*You're* the liar. *You're* the one sneaking around. You promised me honesty. A life together... and all the while you were building this... this web of deceit. And now you stand there and talk to me like *I'm* the problem?"

His composure cracked. "You think this marriage has been easy?" His voice rose. The first true edge of anger she'd heard in months. Maybe that was the only genuine reaction he had exhibited in years. "You think you're the only one who's suffered? You have *no idea* what I've been carrying, what I've sacrificed."

"Sacrificed? Nights with your mistress? The lies? The experiments?" She stepped closer. "What have you really sacrificed, Aubrey... your conscience? Your soul? I think someone with 3 fucking kids would have an answer. How many years have you led my stupid ass on pretending you wanted a future with me? That wasn't *my* choice, dear husband."

His eyes nearly popped out of his skull when she mentioned *children*. "I... I... I don't know what you're talking about." His eyes were wild and full of disbelief. She kind of liked seeing his smug smirk disintegrate.

It just felt so good to let everything go. Apparently, he was just expecting her to be as she always was. No. No more. For the first time in recollection, she actually *got* to *him*. That had never happened. He always had some snide, snarky low blow she didn't expect. He always had the last word and the last say. She continued. "What a lovely family photograph you have on your desk. So... Am *I* the other woman... Or is she?"

He grappled to regain his usual composure. Badly. She didn't stop, "Leigh, isn't it? She good with the whole having another woman as your wife?"

He raked a hand through his hair, exasperated, and turned away. He scrambled to regain control. "You don't understand," he muttered.

"Oh, indeed, I do not." she spat. "Because right now, all I see is a greedy, two-faced coward. But what do I know? I'm practically *unraveling*, aren't I?"

She knew she shouldn't have admitted what she heard. She should've told the attorney first. But, at that second, she was secretly elated. He went completely pale. His eyes grew so wide they barely seemed human. She didn't want to stop. She could grow to like it. "I guess the neighbor will be a good witness when I really lose it, huh?" She hissed.

It was as effective as a punch to the gut. For a long moment, he said nothing. The house seemed to hold its breath. The faint sizzle of the antique lamp, a single pulse of light crossing his face, just enough for her to see that he was trembling. She had to bite her lip to suppress her smile.

When he spoke, his voice was small. "I can't imagine what you mean... I don't know...." he said. The raw honesty in his tone stopped her cold. It wasn't an excuse. It was worse, an emptiness. The truth stripped bare.

Her anger softened into despair. "I loved you," she said quietly. "Even when it hurt. Even when you gave me nothing. But I don't know you. I don't know if I ever did."

His face was still pale as she stared at him. The corners of his mouth twitched like he wanted to say something but couldn't.

"No—" she cut him off. "No, apologies. I just want to know *why?*"

Aubrey looked down. The silence stretched. When he finally spoke, it was barely a whisper. "Why not?" For a heartbeat, the room darkened, just slightly. Enough to make the air feel heavier. This was the real Aubrey now. Cold. Greedy. Gone.

She took a step back. The realization dawning cold and sharp. The man she loved really was gone. She swallowed hard and continued, "So, please tell me, *why* am I unraveling?"

Aubrey's eyes flicked toward the door, a small, guilty motion. He was desperate to leave. Her pulse spiked. "What have you done?"

He turned away again. He stared through the glass into the dark yard below. "Nothing you need to know about."

The lamp went out, then buzzed back on. Down the hall, a faint sound echoed, a single creak, followed by another. Slow, deliberate, pacing footsteps. She didn't say anything to him this time. Could he even hear them? Or was it just her? He scrambled to get his fresh clothes on as quickly as possible.

The air seemed to thicken, vibrating faintly around them. Aubrey's eyes darted to the ceiling, his expression unreadable. She stepped closer to him out of instinct. She stepped back and barely masked the tremble in her voice. "Aubrey, do you hear something?"

He didn't answer. The overhead light flickered. Once, twice, then went out. For a moment, there was nothing, only their breathing, and the low hum of the house.

Then came a whisper, faint and distant, from somewhere beyond the door: "Need help."

Her stomach dropped. Aubrey's expression didn't change. If anything, he looked... resigned. The house groaned, the sound rose from the walls themselves. She clutched her arms to her chest. Her pulse roared in her ears.

"Aubrey," she whispered, "what have you done?"

But he didn't answer. He just turned away from her again, his reflection faint in the darkened glass. He finished gathering some things and said he needed time. Fine. So did she. As a matter of fact, he had the rest of his life.

Chapter 17

She sat on the edge of the bed. The folder clutched to her chest like a talisman. Her mind spiraled off into of half-formed thoughts of fear and revenge. The house was still now, no creaks, no sighs, only that dense silence, pregnant with anticipation.

The folder was in the mystery box, at the bottom. She'd been working on deciphering it for hours. it was full of jargon and nomenclature. It was a patient study, a female patient. She would understand it, one way or another. It was urgent. She didn't understand why, but she knew she had to.

She felt him still, the boy, somewhere nearby. Not gone. Watching. She also felt something dark somewhere. Maybe they were a group package, and you had to have one to have the other.

She didn't know what Aubrey meant when he declared he needed some time to get himself together. He had years to do that before. If anything, *she* needed time.

Either way, he was gone, and she felt relief. HE would probably come back if she said anything, so she would keep that to herself. For once, she just didn't care. In retrospect, she really hadn't cared in years. There was nothing to save. Nothing to salvage. It was remarkably freeing to admit it.

She did like how he never overcame her mentioning *unraveling*. She had found the only way she knew of to get under his skin. But why? She didn't like what that might mean.

She opened the folder again, unable to stop herself. The pages fluttered like trapped birds. The words scrawled across them jittery and frantic. it was Aubrey's handwriting, but it wasn't. The margins of Aubrey's paperwork were filled with looping notes that grew smaller, more chaotic, as though written in panic.

PSYCHOLOGICAL INSTABILITY.
AUDITORY MANIFESTATIONS.
IRREVERSIBLE SIDE EFFECTS.

Her eyes caught on a single line.

SUBJECT REPORTS SEEING FIGURES IN
PERIPHERAL VISION, UNABLE TO DISCERN
IF THEY ARE REAL OR IMAGINED.

Her breath caught. She slammed the folder shut and held it to her chest. She didn't know why that was so powerful but the weight of it pressed on her like the house's air when it was angry, thick, damp, suffocating.

The silence deepened. Her feet moved before her mind caught up. They carried her down the hallway. The air was colder here. The shadows moved with a slow, liquid rhythm, as if they were breathing.

The home's silence was strange. It seemed to come and go of its own accord as time passed. It could just be her. Could be that bug, whatever it was. Some days she felt like she was developing the flu. Some days it felt like a sinus infection. She had periods of chilling but never had a fever. Nausea that came and went. Weakness and fatigue that could disappear within an hour or so.

Her physician was no help in the matter. He tested for everything he could think of. She wasn't pregnant, had no infections, and no signs of illness. He attributed everything to allergies that could be from anything. A new environment. Residual construction materials from the renovations. Any change in cleaning products or ingredients. It could also be a new allergy to something in her daily life. He wrote her a prescription for allergy medication and advised her to call the office if anything changed. The allergy medication hadn't done anything.

Strangely, the guest room door was half open. Again. She usually kept it closed to keep the dust contained. She hadn't started the second phase of renovating yet. The upstairs guest rooms were on the list of things to do. Just like the small rooms in back of the first floor.

There was so much going on in her life. She missed her routine. She missed simple pleasures. She missed her oblivion. Even ignorant bliss was still bliss. She rarely saw him anyway, so what did any of it matter?

She hesitated, then pushed it open. The room exhaled a draft of cold air that smelled faintly of damp soil and stone. The mirror across from the bed loomed larger than she remembered, its glass no longer reflective but opaque, clouded with a slow, pulsing fog.

Not again, she thought. She was tired of the unexplained. She wanted nice, calm, boring routine. Aubrey didn't have to be part of it. He never was before. She didn't expect him to be just because they moved.

The fog in the glass shifted. She slowly approached it. The image morphed into something. The strange shape looked almost like a lung. Her fingertips grazed the glass. The surface quivered and rippled like it was made of water. She probably shouldn't be so close. She slowly backed away.

And then, he was there. The boy's pale face emerged from the fog, eyes dark and endless. He didn't blink. Didn't breathe. Just watched her with that same unbearable sorrow, as if *he* knew what she was about to see.

"Who are you?" she whispered. Her breath fogged in the newly frigid air. "What do you want from me?"

He didn't answer. He lifted one hand and pointed, not at her or the mirror, but at the bed. She turned. Something protruded from beneath the mattress. It was a corner of paper, yellowed and brittle. It was nearly identical to the dusty linens around it.

It was an old piece of paper. It was brittle and left a faint residue on her fingertips, as though coated in dust older than the house itself. It looked ancient. The ink was faint, spider-thin, written in a precise, delicate hand.

It wasn't a letter. It was a list on old ledger paper.

Umbra Infesta Patient Log

PATIENT ONE — FAILED
PATIENT TWO — UNSTABLE
PATIENT THREE — VANISHED
PATIENT FOUR — SEE NOTES (TOTAL
CEREBRAL DETERIORATION)
PATIENT FIVE — UNKNOWN

Her throat constricted. The edges of the page trembled in her grip. Why did it feel so similar to Aubreys notes? These weren't names, but they were *lives*. And each line on that page was a death sentence. She didn't understand how she knew it. The page contained the same information for 25 people. All of them had the same outcomes.

Aubrey's lab conducted human experiments. She'd gathered that from the paperwork. She wondered how many victims he'd known. Even if the lab had proper documentation, human experimentation seemed so wrong.

The mirror behind her pulsed again with a muffled thud. She turned. The fog had parted, the boy gone. In his place, something darker stirred, a shape. A shadow that didn't belong to anything human. Its outline warped and transformed. A constant shift between form and void, as though it struggled to exist.

It watched her. The room felt too small. The air too thin. She felt faint, like the shadow in the mirror was draining the oxygen from the room.

She stumbled backward. The parchment page slipped from her hand. She hit the doorframe. The impact brought her out of the fog. She bolted out of the room and slammed the door behind her. Her back pressed to the wood, her chest heaving.

Silence. Then, faintly, from inside the room, a soft scratching. It sounded like fingernails tracing the mirror's surface, like they were sliding down an old chalkboard. She clamped her hands over her ears. "Stop," she whispered. "Please, stop."

But the sound wasn't outside anymore. It was *inside* her. Maybe it was always inside her. Maybe she was *unraveling*, like Aubrey said. Maybe everything she experienced was in her head.

She ran to her bedroom and collapsed onto the bed. She closed her eyes a moment and tried to relax. It wasn't easy. She had so many questions. Questions about the house. About what Aubrey was doing. What was the purpose? What did he know? Why would she be going crazy?

Sure, finding out about his mistress and possible children was traumatizing, but it's not like they were a normal couple. In any way. They were far closer to frenemies than spouses, and that was on good days. There wasn't much left to be traumatized by. She'd hoped he was returning to his old self when they moved in, but she never had enough evidence to fully accept it.

She looked over to the nightstand. The patient list from now sat on the nightstand, silent and unassuming. She could feel it, its weight, its pulse. She hadn't put it there. She knew that much. She left it in the old room.

The house was quiet. Still. She crept down the hall and back to the room. There was no trace of the earlier demonstration. She lifted the ancient featherbed to see what else might be hidden. She didn't find anything... at first. Some bunched up lace turned out to be an ancient handkerchief.

Under that was a stunning vintage photograph in an ornate frame. It was the little boy. She would put that in her room. Several letters were underneath it. They were all addressed to far off locations, but none appeared have any stamps or postal marks.

The letters were never mailed. Maybe whoever it had died before they could be mailed. Maybe.

Chapter 18

She took all the new materials to the study. The old papers were frail. She would store them in a different drawer. She cleaned the frame with the little boy and put it on her dresser. it just seemed like it belonged there.

She pulled the blinds in the den and put music on the television. She kept the letters out. They were addressed to women in North Carolina and several other states. The first was to a woman named Christine. it read:

Dearest Christine,

I miss you so. Reyland has put me in his clinic. I believe he means to kill me. By the time you get this, I may already be gone. Do not come here. He's going to marry Esmeralda, the nurse I felt so sorry for. I feel so foolish.

He blames me for Charlie's death. I think his trying to hide his own guilt for killing him.

You've been a wonderful sister. I was going to come and live with you all, like you suggested in your last letter. Then, Charlie got sick. After he passed, I did the same. I thought it was just a cold when it started. I now think Reyland did it. Just know, if I don't survive, I will be with my boy. What more can I ask for?

I love you and will await our reunion, in this life, or in Heaven.

The mood of the letter was so despondent. She heard a rumble outside. She peeked out of the blinds. The sky was dark and angry.

She felt some of the letter's despondency. She had an awful feeling that she might be writing a letter like that herself one day. When she had unraveled. When there was nothing left.

She looked at the next letter, to Cousin Adaline in Ohio:

My dearest Adaline,

I pray this letter reaches you while it still matters, before the last of my strength slips through my fingers. You and I have always been bound by something more than blood, two halves of a childhood stitched together with secrets, laughter, and the stubbornness of women determined not to stay in place. I find myself thinking of those days often now. They feel like a distant season, one I can recall but no longer touch.

I will not waste your time with pleasantries; I have so little left. What I must tell you is terrible, and I know it will frighten you. But I cannot leave this world, if that is indeed what awaits, without placing the truth in the hands of the one person who has never doubted me.

Adaline, something is wrong with this house. And something is even more wrong with my husband.

You knew Reyland as I once did, brilliant, charming, beloved by the town for his skill with the infirm. You would scarcely recognize him now. The change has been gradual, like ivy slowly consuming a stone wall, until suddenly nothing beneath remains visible. He spends his nights in the cellar laboratory, locked away with his instruments and papers, refusing me entry even when I beg. His patients are in the attic, if you can call them that. He seldom visits and never treats.

I have gone down there only once. Once was enough. I cannot describe everything I saw, for even now my hand shakes at the memory.

Jars of things that should not have been preserved. Strange diagrams pinned to the walls, all circling a figure drawn in thick, frantic charcoal, something bent and elongated, like a man who had been stretched until human shape no longer fit him. And the smell, Adaline... the smell of earth and rot, like a grave unearthed.

But the worst part was Reyland himself. He looked at me as though I were a specimen, something to categorize, to dissect, to understand. His eyes shone with a feverish light I have never seen in any mortal man. He spoke of "binding" and "inviting," of a force older than the foundations of this earth. He said fear itself had form, and he meant to give it a body.

Since that night, I think the house has awakened. I hear whispers through the walls, though no one is there. The floors breathe beneath my feet. Drafts move against me in the shape of fingers. Charlie used to cry in his sleep, saying the "tall man" watches him from the corners. I soothed him then, but now... now I fear he speaks the truth.

I have written to doctors, to clergy, even to Reyland's colleagues. No one answers. Perhaps he intercepts them. Perhaps he has already turned them all against me.

I know what people may assume, that grief and isolation have rotted my senses. But, Adaline, you must believe me. You must. If anything happens to me, do not let the world call it illness. Do not let Reyland write my death off as the collapse of a fragile mind. I am more sound than I have ever been, for terror has a way of sharpening reality.

He is doing something down there. Something that warps the house. Something that hollows the light from his eyes and fills him with shadows.

If I should disappear, or if word reaches you that my heart failed, know this: it will not be from natural causes.

I fear Reyland means to make me part of his work, a vessel for whatever he has brought into this place.

Please take this letter and keep it safe. Tell someone, anyone, who will listen.

The shadows watch me even now. I feel them gather in the corners of the room as I write. Time is short, and courage shorter.

Remember me kindly, Adaline.
Remember who I was before this darkness took root.

With all the love I have left,

Allura

She returned the letters to their respective drawer. She fiddled with Aubrey's papers again. She didn't want to be in her situation. She didn't want to unravel. She could ignore it all, but that wouldn't change anything. It would just leave her vulnerable.

She placed Allura's papers in a different drawer of the desk in the study. It locked along with the drawer where her cache of documents were.

She signed and flipped through those again. She found receipts from two Christmases earlier. He visited New York City with his mistress and left her alone at home. She visited Francis to celebrate... if you could call it that. They had both seen better holidays. There was also a science convention he didn't actually go to. He took his mistress to Cabo.

She felt bitter, but she was bitter long before the evidence. Every word inside the paperwork was a seed, and whatever situation he planted now bloomed in the dark. It was a dark and frightening garden.

She flipped through the papers. How did Francis get them? She flipped through its contents. If the dates had been different on the contents of that box, they could've been from their dating life.

Her favorite restaurants, lingerie shops, even the hotels they frequented, once upon a time. It was so strange. Maybe those were really his favorite places, and he just let her think she enjoyed them. She didn't know how much of her current interests were really her interests, and not interesting because of Aubrey.

She thought of his face when she confronted him, the flicker of guilt, the fatigue in his voice. The realization that the man she married was just gone. That hurt her the most. She could overlook even his current assholery... if that man still existed, somewhere. But he didn't. It was like a death.

Her stomach twisted. It was better to get away from him as soon as possible. She returned to the papers to their respective drawer. She couldn't think of old Aubrey. Old Aubrey was dead, if he ever existed. She hadn't admitted it, but deep down, she had known for a long time. She had to keep her eyes forward.

She began thinking of the little boy. Was his plea just a warning? What if it was a memory? Was the little boy part of that patient group on the ledger paper? Why would he be warning her? People got divorced every day. There was no real threat of anything dangerous. He must've been Charlie.

She looked at the mirror across the room. Her own reflection appeared faint and distorted in the dark. For a moment, she thought she saw him again, standing just behind her shoulder. A flash of pale skin. A whisper of movement. Then it was gone.

She pressed her hands to her face. A new and frightening thought came to mind. The thought clawed at her mind. *What if it's not the house? What if it's me?* Was she the one doing the haunting? Could the haunted house really be just in her mind?

The house groaned around her. Its timbers flexed in a long, slow exhale as if to answer her. That didn't help. The house could communicate if it were haunted, but she could also be hearing things. Maybe she needed security cameras. They recorded visuals and sound. She would look into it.

Aubrey called to say he needed to pick up some clothes. She dreaded it. Her attorney said to go about life normally until everything was ready. No one in Aubreys immediate family had ever been divorced. She assumed a myriad of attorneys would come after her to bully her into silence. And compliance. But even as she thought it, she knew the truth. Fleeing was not an option.

Chapter 19

Aubrey seemed drained while he was there. Pale. Strange. She tried to watch television while he gathered what he needed. There wasn't anything much to say. He didn't make any effort to talk to her either.

She was shocked to find he'd checked the water softener and took the trash out. They were such mundane tasks. It seemed out of place. Did all cheating husbands come home to take the trash out? Why would he bother?

He left without saying anything. She didn't know he was gone until she looked out and saw his car was gone. She ambled through the now empty home. A sadness rose in her. She was angry with herself for crying, but she cried anyway. She hadn't cried for him in so long she couldn't remember the last time. She didn't know why she was now.

She had so many questions and there was no hope for an answer. Why hadn't he just asked her for a divorce? Why the move? Why go through such drastic changes instead of the simpler ones? Thunder rolled again outside. Rains had set in for what felt like forever. She dried her eyes and tried to calm herself.

She had such high hopes when they moved in. That maybe the worst was over. That maybe they did have some kind of future. They didn't. All those years meant nothing.

She popped some popcorn and returned to the television. She needed to call James. He asked her to call every few days just to check in. The weather was colder now, and harvest time was over. She missed it. Carefree, peaceful evenings of just talking to a friend.

Pacing started overhead. She already locked the house up, so she knew no one had come in. She walked towards the sound. It could be the little boy. It could also be the scary entity, but it was usually the child. The darkness just followed him.

She walked up to the second floor, but the sound was higher. It was in the attic. She debated on whether or not she would go upstairs.

She needed to finish the renovation but dawdled. She couldn't decide what she wanted to work on. Aubrey lost interest before the first floor was completed. The only room she'd had changed on the second floor was the master bedroom and en suite.

The other rooms had plenty of cheap modern crap left by previous owners, which she would donate or throw away. The real issues came from the old stuff. There were genuine antiques and truly beautiful items, gorgeous furniture, beautiful photographs in scrolling gilded frames. She didn't have a family, but she could imagine they were her people. Those would need to be handled with caution.

She moved up the stairs to the attic. The sound was coming from the back. There were a couple of closets in the back. At least she thought they were closets. She navigated trunks and old towers of cardboard boxes. The floor was coated with a thick layer of dust. Cobwebs hung from the ceiling in such thick tendrils they looked more like dark tentacles.

She followed the sound and opened the door to the closet on the right. It wasn't a closet it at all. There were trunks and stacks of old, musty books inside. The little boy stood in there. She walked in and sat on the trunk by the ancient desk. He watched her without blinking.

"Hi." she softly spoke. That shadow was probably nearby, but he didn't run this time.

"Hi."

"What's your name?"

"Charlie."

"I'm Gabby."

"I know."

They went back and forth for some time. She used the softest voice she could, at first. Eventually, she spoke normally. He called the shadow presence, "Father."

Father didn't come to the attic. That was the realm of his failure. Of his disappointments. Her heart went out to him. He was so small. He was 5 when he died. Father was once a doctor. Charlie contracted fever and died.

"He doesn't like you snooping." Charlie warned. "He doesn't like anyone snooping."

Father's work meant everything to him. More than his wife. More than his son. He believed his experiments would impact humanity. She just listened while he talked about things no child should have to discuss.

It made horrible sense, but it was also alarming. Her husband was also a doctor obsessed with his research. Did Aubrey know? Maybe he planned it from the beginning. She heard whispers from the call she wasn't supposed to hear, *"She's unraveling...."*

Charlie said she should never let him hurt her. She was unable to reply. She didn't know it he meant Father or Aubrey. She wouldn't... if she could help it. She just didn't know what she was up against.

What happened to her life? It was so simple before. Was she being targeted by a ghost... or a husband? Both? She must be the only woman in the world dealing with two angry men, both living and dead. She didn't need to do anything more than exist to fuel their rage.

There was also the issue that Charlie could just be a figment of her imagination. It was possible. But, if such a thing were possible, how? Did Aubrey do something to her? But he was never here. If she were a test subject, someone should be watching her. *If there was no observation, there was no study*, at least according to Aubrey.

Charlie gave her a drawing. It was a picture of him and what appeared to be his mother. Opposite them was a black shadow form with white eyes. That must've been Father. She looked back up to ask him what it meant or why he gave it to her, but he was gone.

She hadn't explored much of the attic since they moved in. It was locked and there was no sign of a key. A locksmith had to open it to preserve the ornate handle and pull plate. Maybe most of it was original.

It had to be a medical practice of some sort at one time. There were primitive cots stacked against one wall. Antique fabric partitions that separated the beds were folded beside them. Everything had a thick coating of dust and cobwebs. Dusty shelves were lined with moldy files and paper. She needed to inventory those rooms before she thought of renovating. Maybe the historical society would have some use for the old stuff.

The lights up here flickered and spat. She wiped off the window and looked out. She could see beyond Murkwood. She had the perfect perch for a blackmailer. She watched the houses below a moment. No signs of life anywhere. The yards in front were as empty as the pools out back. *So much for blackmailing.*

She returned downstairs for a drink. She was exhausted. Maybe she just needed more sleep. She returned to the television. She stretched out on the sectional couch. She grabbed a throw quilt and settled in.

She needed to go to the library. That was another change that had thrown her since the move. She used to visit the library several days a week. She was a voracious reader. Did they even have a library in Murkwood?

She turned on the crafting channel and relaxed. The worries of the world faded into background noise. She thought she heard a multitude of whispers gather round her but decided it was just the residue of the television. She drew comfort from the fact that Charlie watched over her. She might not have an actual child, but she still had one in a small sense. Or she could be crazy. She could be unraveling.

Chapter 20

The house didn't groan or sigh anymore. It seemed to listen. After Charlie vanished, the silence that followed wasn't relief so much as a held note, taut and breathless. Like the walls themselves waited to see what she would do with what she now knew.

It's safer up here, he had whispered. His small face pale and intent. His eyes flicked toward the ceiling. *Father doesn't like the attic. He doesn't come this high if he can help it.* The word felt thin in her mouth, like tissue paper. *Safe.* But it was more than she had yesterday, and more than she'd had in months.

Shadows lay in mild folds along the baseboards. The air had the faint, old sweetness of cedar and dust. She switched on the bedside lamp, then switched it off again. The ambient dusk made the room cozy. Night pressed on the windows like a listening ear.

She tried to sleep and failed. Her body remembered how, but her mind moved in clean, bright flashes: the boy's voice, the temperature drop, the tremor of certainty that what he said was true. There was a logic to the house if she held still long enough. There were rules. The attic, Charlie had said. Father avoided the attic.

Near midnight, another sound began. At first it was indistinct, the kind of thing an exhausted mind invents: a soft, dry whisper, not unlike leaves against brick. She barely noticed it. Then it steadied. *Scritch.* Pause. *Scritch.* Measured like knitting needles. Deliberate as scratching on a tabletop.

She sat up, every sense sharp as if someone had rinsed her in cold water. Her feet found the floorboards cool, slightly ridged with age. The old house's night scent rose around her: stale heat, old varnish, that faint metallic tang she could never place. She pulled on her oversized robe, slid her palms together to steady the tremor, and took the flashlight from the nightstand drawer.

The hallway reminded her of a pulse. The air followed the pattern. The wallpaper's faded blossoms floated pale in the low light. The scratching continued, never frantic, never panicked, just the stubborn insistence of something that wished to be counted. She stood to chase it.

Not the guest room, no, not the hall. It was above her head again. Higher than the flat run of ceiling over the second floor. Not from the crawlspace door by the linen closet, but beyond that. In the wide-bellied dark of the attic itself.

She touched the banister. The cool wood seemed to hold a thin thread of early winter. The attic stairs waited behind the narrow door at the end. Its brass knob cold and slightly damp under her hand. She half expected it to resist. It turned without complaint.

The first step groaned. The second announced itself. The third fell into silence as she learned the weight that wouldn't provoke protest.

She climbed in that slow rhythm. One hand on the wall, the other carrying the flashlight low. Its beam swept across the close, angled geometry of the stairwell. Dust drifted, slow as snow in the cone of light. Something in the wood whispered, resin, old glue, maybe old air waking.

She wandered again through the maze and went to an area previously unexplored. She came to a door that was apparently meant to be hidden. It gave her a terrible feeling. It blended into the wall seamlessly. She reached for it and braced herself. The panel moved with a papery sigh, and a cool current slithered over her skin. It smelled faintly of dried flowers and the spent sweetness of mothballs. Her breath fogged faintly.

This part of the attic was a long, low-bellied room stitched by rafters. The ceiling was cut into angles by the roofline. Moonlight crept through one small dormer and laid pale light across a trunk and the floor beyond. Covered shapes stood like resting animals under yellowed sheets. An armoire, two chairs, a laundry rack. The flashlight beam slid across everything. It painted surfaces briefly into being, then let them go.

Scritch. The sound came again. This time from her right. Faintly ahead, a slice of wall broken by a row of small, built-in cupboards. Their low doors set into the eaves where the roof dipped close to the floor. There were three, identical, plain, painted the same aged cream as the trim downstairs.

She walked toward them. Each step was soft and dry. As the beam crawled across the room, a slight draft wavered against her knuckles. The first closet's latch looked painted shut, the edges sealed by decades of lazy brushes and ancient latex paint. The second bore a stain near the base, water maybe, created a line faint and brown as tea. *Scritch.* Pause. *Scritch.* From behind the third door, like a beetle in a jar.

Dust lay unbroken in most places, but there, along the seam at the bottom. A thin crescent was brushed clean by air moving where it shouldn't. Her mouth dried. She laid her fingers along the seam and the door answered with a tiny shiver, as if it had nerves and recognized her touch.

"Charlie?" she breathed. Silence. Then, a slight breeze carried the smallest sigh.

The latch was a simple turn of nickel gone dull. At least it wasn't coated in paint. It resisted first, then gave with a sticky click. The residual paint cracked like sugar. The door swung three reluctant inches. Cold air exhaled from the dark, layered with old cedar and something sweeter, like the end of roses.

"No farther," she told herself softly, though the words weren't her own. They were instinct, or Charlie, or some ragged thread of common sense she hadn't utterly burned. "Just look."

She eased the strange door open. The interior was a wedge of space where the roof sank low. Rough boards made the floor, boards again on the back wall. A single shelf ran along the left, empty save for a small shape tucked into the far corner.

Her beam found it: a knitted thing, child-small and puckered with moth holes. A mitten. Pale blue, dulled by attic light. She let the beam rest there, and the whole room felt a fraction colder.

As she approached, she saw the back wall wasn't flush. Where the boards met the left side, a slim blister of air darkened the seam. The fit was wrong. The closet had a back, and then another.

She flattened her palm against the boards. She sat the flashlight sit on the floor, angling it to rake light across the seams. The boards weren't original; the nails differed, newer by some decades, their heads too uniform, too bright beneath their rust. A panel, then. A panel that had been added. A panel that could be removed.

Her hands steadied. She slid her fingers into the small black slit at the seam, but the gap narrowed groin-tight where the wood had swelled. She probed the inner edge and felt, not nail, not smooth board, metal. A small circle recessed into the wood like a coin pressed halfway, no larger than a cuff button.

"Come on," she murmured. She reached into her robe pocket for the only tool she had: the dull edge of a key to a lock she never found. She pushed its tip into the circle and felt it catch in a thin slit. Not a coin. A keyhole. Painted over, hidden on purpose, a mouth made to keep shut.

She swallowed air that tasted like the inside of old trunks. She tried the key anyway, likely futile, but with hope. It didn't fit. She laughed once under her breath, the sound too loud, too human. Of course not. The house wouldn't open because she asked nicely. It would open because it had decided she was ready to see or because she made it yield.

She slid the flashlight farther into the closet to widen her light and something on the floor flashed back. A small, off-hand glint from a scatter of dust. Not light, exactly, just a suggestion of it.

She set her palm down to balance and felt grit cling to her skin, fine as flour. Her fingers found the glint: a slender length of metal half-buried, no longer than a matchstick. She rubbed it clean on her robe. A delicate skeleton key came free, thin as a stitch, cold as forgotten coins in snow.

Her breath shook the dust. She looked at the key and felt the house shuffle closer, as if it had moved its chair an inch nearer.

"Okay," she said to the air, to the boy, to herself.

The key slid into the small round opening as if the two were made to match. It stopped. She twisted. Resistance; then a soft, inward click. The panel did not fall open. It wasn't a door in a children's book, and she felt foolish relief at that. Instead, the right side of the boards moved back the smallest breath. The seam widened by the width of a fingernail.

Cold breathed out, damp earth, old paper, traces of something too old to name. Her eyes stung suddenly, a mean little prick at the corners, as if the air in there had missed air.

She worked her fingers into the seam and pulled. The panel came forward an inch, then another, then stopped hard against the inner framing. She shifted grip, tugged low, then high. It eased, grudgingly, like something too long asleep. She managed three inches of blackness, then four. Enough to slide her hand in up to the wrist. Not enough to see.

"Don't... rush." Charlie's voice, or memory of it, brushed her ear. It could have been the words themselves. It could have been the cool air on her neck where no window should have breathed.

She crouched and pressed her cheek near the seam. She peered in with one eye. The flashlight washed the inner space white as a slice of bone. She blinked the dust from her eyes and saw shapes, flat stacks, cloth edges, the blurred geometry of boxes. The light struck something that threw it back in dull silver: a frame? A hinge?

Her hand reached in, and her fingers met paper, loosely wrapped. Cloth covered it, soft and slightly oily with time. The sort of dark linen people used to call cambric, often found in the backs of catalogs.

She pinched the corner and felt the weight of it. It yielded under her touch and whispered against the side of the opening, not a threatening whisper but the sound of paper sliding against itself.

She withdrew her hand as if shocked, heart quick, mouth full of pennies. The attic felt abruptly closer, rafters lowering like cathedral ribs. The quiet that followed was almost devout.

"This is where you put it," she said under her breath, though she hadn't meant to. "This is where you hid it from him."

From the rafters, something cracked. Wood settled like a back straightening after a long sit. The house's temperature rose by some mercy of physics or sentiment, and for a moment, the attic smelled like... soap, almost. Sun-bleached cotton.

She could rip the panel the rest of the way free. Summon the raw strength and leverage the boards until they gave. She could. The part of her that survived on command urged it. But another voice, maybe older than this house, a sensible girl's voice from a room with a low window and a quilt, said *relax.*

She eased the panel back into place. The small click of the latch sliding home sounded like relief. She slipped the key into her pocket and left the mitten where it was.

On hands and knees, she backed out of the closet. Dust gathered in pale crescents on her jeans. She sat on the attic floor and let the flashlight lie. Its beam painted the door, its light thinning at the edges.

A draft passed her shoulder, cool and cautious. She turned and, just for a moment, saw the shape of a boy. He stood in the slender sash of moonlight, not fully made. She could only see the impression of him, the tilt of his head, the small square of his shoulders. He didn't approach. He didn't need to.

"Tomorrow," she spoke with a steady voice.

Charlie didn't nod, but the sense of assent hovered. The attic, so recently an animal poised to startle, loosened in its joints, and the slow chorus of the house resumed, the far murmur of pipes. The soft sound of wind catching on slate. An owl's distant call.

102

She rose. The floorboard beneath her right foot complained, but the next board held. She crossed back to the door and left the ghosts in the attic to guard her discovery.

The second floor welcomed her with air that had known human habitation. She closed the attic door and set her palm briefly against its paint. The wood held a mild warmth that she made herself ignore. There was nothing in there to get warm. It had to be her. Or the house. She walked away.

She took a shower to get rid of the dust. Steam fogged the mirror to a soft bloom. She watched herself appear through it as the glass cleared: her eyes brighter than yesterday, the corners of her mouth primed for lines that weren't grief.

She slid into bed without turning on the lamp. Sleep came, not all at once but in increments, as if the body had to negotiate its return. When it found her, it was dark and untroubled.

Once, in the middle hours, she woke at the feel of a pressure at the mattress's edge, feather-light, like the weight of a book or a small hand briefly testing the give of fabric. She didn't move. She wasn't afraid, she was just too exhausted to acknowledge it. The pressure eventually lifted.

Dawn bathed the house in tender colors, the kind of gray that blushes as it loses itself to light. When she opened her eyes, the first thing she saw was the thin line of sun along the top seam of the curtains.

For a moment, she was young again, the day promising itself without condition. She started to search for a trinket she kept back then but hadn't remembered since.

It was a fake sapphire ring she'd gotten from a bubble gum machine. She kept it until it was just a sliver of plasticky "metal" and a dull, vaguely blue blob. She couldn't remember why it was so important. One of her foster families threw it out. She had several foster families; each worse than the last.

She looked at her hands. She wore diamonds now. Very real. Very expensive. Aubrey ensured she had jewelry that matched his "status." Wouldn't want people to talk. There was nothing worse than a wealthy miser, was there? She didn't love any of them as much as that first one, even if she couldn't recall why she'd loved that toy.

She rose with the quiet satisfaction of someone who has already chosen her next action. She put on her robe, slid the key out of her pocket, and stepped into the hall. She filled a travel tumbler with hot coffee and ascended the steps.

The attic door waited for her. The fresh paint had cured to eggshell, for now. Its beautiful brass knob faintly tarnished. She thought she heard a single soft footstep above, no menace, only a gentle pace heard when you start to enter a room.

"Okay," she said to the house, to the boy, to the woman who had written in a hand like water slipping downhill. "I'm coming."

And the house, which had quietly breathed around secrets, breathed in. The day took hold. The key in her pocket, small and cold, pressed it against her thigh, and the future narrowed, clean and bright as a cut.

Chapter 21

She felt the draft before she saw it make the old papers flutter. A faint exhale of air from the cracked panel, cool and stale, as if the house had held its breath for a century. Dust hung in the beam of her lantern. Motes trembled like insects caught mid-flight. Every movement sent faint whispers across the wood, dry sighs of paper, the groan of old nails shifting in their sockets.

The bundle now lay before her on a crooked table. It was tied in faded ribbon the color of old bones. Its corners were soft from handling. Whatever was inside had been touched often, not forgotten, merely hidden.

She untied the knot. A smell unfurled: mildew, iron, wax, and something faintly sweet beneath, like lavender. She didn't recognize it, but it made her throat tighten.

Inside the bundle were letters, loose sheets of notes, and at the very center, a small blue diary with frayed edges. The initials **A.H.** were pressed into the cover, faded but still visible under the lantern light. For a moment, she thought of all the documents Francis presented to her.

"Allura Hayes," she whispered, tasting the name. It felt foreign and familiar at once, like a word she'd heard in a dream. She opened the diary. The pages crackled faintly as though in protest. Its edges browned to the color of tea. A pressed sprig of something, rosemary or thyme, crumbled to dust between the first two pages.

April 3rd, 1924

Reyland says the attic is perfect for his practice. "High ceilings, ample light, privacy." That word unsettles me. He means privacy from the hospital board, of course, but lately I think he also means privacy from me.

He calls his studies "work of the mind," though lately he speaks of it as if it were scripture. He says the human brain is a gate, half-closed, that fear or fever can force it open.

I told him not everything that can be seen is meant to be seen. He laughed, kissed my cheek, and said I sounded like the nurses who gossip about ghosts.

She looked up from the page. The shadows along the rafters seemed closer, sloping inward. They were drawn toward her small circle of light. She rubbed her arms. The air had grown damp and cool. It carried that faint lavender smell again, stronger this time, tinged with something metallic.

She turned another page.

April 18th, 1924

Reyland works all night now. The attic murmurs when he is down in his laboratory, a low vibration in the beams. Charlie says he hears Father talking to someone even when no one answers back.

He says they whisper through the light. That sometimes, when the lamps flicker, he sees faces in the corners.

Reyland calls them projections of the subconscious. He says the brain can be trained to see the "unlit world" if fear is sharpened enough.

I said I don't want Charlie anywhere near that kind of sight. He told me I am holding back human progress.

Her pulse climbed. Her fingers itched to turn the next page, but part of her didn't want to know what came next. It played on her own fears. The lantern flame trembled, not from draft, but from a pulse in the air, as if the attic had a heartbeat of its own.

She read on.

May 6th, 1925

Charlie is ill. A fever came upon him so quickly. His cheeks are the color of glass, his pulse too slow. Reyland will not call for our usual physician; he insists he can treat him here. He says illness lowers the veil, that the body's weakness lets the mind open wider.

I begged him to stop. He asked if I wanted Charlie to die a coward's death, blind, unawakened.

I slapped him. I've never struck anyone before. He smiled when I did it. He said anger is the truest doorway of all.

I think I would die with Charlie. Most women are on their third or fourth child by now. Reyland won't stop working long enough to conceive another.

A sound behind her. A soft thud, like a chair leg shifting. She turned. Breath caught in her throat. Nothing but the dark stretched toward the far wall. Yet the shadows seemed to lean slightly toward her, as if they were listening.

She closed the diary halfway but couldn't stop. She had to see. She needed to understand.

May 12th, 1925

Reyland has begun his "trial." He calls it an act of mercy. Our current patients are wards of the state. He said it was perfect because they're just burdens anyway.

It wasn't enough. I suspect he's already ruined my boy. My beautiful son. Charlie's fever broke this morning, but he doesn't speak. He just stares. Sometimes he laughs softly, but not at anything here. He says there are lights moving behind the ceiling boards. That Father made them for him to follow.

When I went to the attic, I found my husband drawing circles in chalk around the table carefully. Perfect circles that whispered faintly when I stepped near.

He told me to go back downstairs. I think there are things in this room that know my name. I think he's going to experiment on me, too.

Her throat burned. The smell of iron was stronger now, unmistakably blood, though she saw none. Her skin prickled with a faint, electric cold.

She skipped ahead to the middle of the book:

July 22nd, 1925

Charlie lingered for two weeks. Two weeks of quiet, broken breaths and that faraway smile that never reached me. He'd stopped recognizing my face by the third day. After that, I think he was already gone.

His eyes followed things I couldn't see, drifting shapes above him. He said sometimes they pulsed with a light. I swear I could feel in my bones but couldn't bear to look. He whispered to them... said they were waiting. When he finally went still, he looked peaceful, like he'd stepped into the space he'd been watching.

I didn't move for days after they took him away. Reyland said he'd "see to the arrangements." I didn't ask what that meant. The house was so quiet I could hear the floorboards breathe. Every time I closed my eyes, I saw my boy's hands, so small, so cold, so precious, and I couldn't tell if I was still awake or dreaming.

Then came the fever. It started with an ache in my back, then the heat behind my eyes. I thought it was grief, but by the second night, I couldn't stand without shaking. Reyland said it was influenza. That he'd take care of me. He told the housekeeper I was to be moved to the clinic, that I'd be "under observation." The way he said it made my skin crawl.

109

I begged to stay in my own bed, but he looked at me the way he looks at his patients. With that same calm disgust, like he's already measuring how long I'll last. He said if I refused, he'd have me declared insane, and I know what that means. The asylum, the endless corridors, the echo of my name called by strangers who never return. After all, who in their right mind would refuse treatment when ill? An insane person.

I hear him moving below the stairs now, gathering his instruments. He mumbles to himself when he works. Sometimes he sings the same tune he used to sing to Charlie when he was small. He never said where he heard it. I want to believe there's still something human left in him, but everything is different now.

I can't get warm. The fever burns but I'm freezing. The attic smells like iron and chalk, and there's light flickering through the cracks again, soft, white, and slow, like it's breathing. I think it's calling my name.

If I don't come back from his clinic, I pray someone finds this. I pray they burn the house.

The diary's last page had a single line scrawled in hurried script, half-torn:

He says the fever unlocked the gate. He says I'll see "Father" too.

The ink had bled down the page in a thin trail, as if the words had wept onto the paper. She shut the diary. The sound of it closing felt too loud. The house gave a tiny creak in answer, a noise like a sigh or a hinge remembering how to move.

She set the diary down gently, afraid to disturb the air again. In the silence that followed, she thought she heard a faint roar, low, rhythmic, from somewhere beneath the floorboards. Like breathing. Or a heartbeat. Or someone whispering her name very, very softly.

She reached for the lantern and froze. A child's handprint, small and gray with dust, marked the far wall, newly pressed, just at her eye level.

Chapter 22

After her encounter, the attic seemed to crouch like a living thing. The support beams groaned faintly through the night. The slow, deliberate creaking felt almost conversational, as though the house disapproved of her trespass.

The words wouldn't leave her. *He says I'll see "Father" too.* The phrase had taken root somewhere deep and replayed whenever the floor shifted or the lights dimmed. Eventually, it no longer sounded like a child's warning but something older.

She spent the hours at dawn just pacing the house. She'd suffered with insomnia forever, but the house seemed to exaggerate it. Her bare feet brushed across the cold floorboards. The air up here carried a faint sweetness, old perfume, maybe, or dust stirred from forgotten linens. She went down to the kitchen to make coffee.

Her mind stayed back in the attic. The smell of dried lavender crushed to powder. The thin rasp of paper under her fingertips. The sense that something unseen had leaned in close while she read.

The boy's voice lingered in the space between her thoughts. Soft as breath. It curled around her name. Sometimes, if she stood perfectly still, she could almost believe he was right beside her. His small fingers clutching the fabric of her sleeve.

By the time she heard the front door open, the morning already burned away through the curtains. The house, silent for hours, stirred at the sound. The clatter of keys on the entry table broke the spell like a slap. Then came the heavy rhythm of Aubrey's footsteps, deliberate and unhurried, rolling through the floorboards like a pulse the house recognized. Each step vibrated faintly under her feet. The air thickened, not with fear exactly, but with something heavy, magnetic. A tension that had become as constant as the creaks in the walls.

"Gabriella?" His voice cut through the hall, sharp, expectant, edged with impatience.

She took a breath to steady her tone. "In the kitchen."

The words felt foreign in her mouth, thin and fragile. She pressed her palms against the countertop. She felt the faint grit of sporadic dust. The coolness of the marble seeped into her skin. When his shadow stretched across the doorway, her stomach drew tight.

Aubrey appeared, pale and drawn. The light caught in his eyes like metal under glass. His movements were clipped, almost mechanical, as if he were remembering how to inhabit his own body. He didn't look at her. Didn't greet her. Just opened the refrigerator and reached for a bottle of water.

"You're late," she said, each word careful, evenly spaced. "Was there a lot going on at the lab?"

For a moment, the air seemed to pause with him. His hand froze mid-reach. "What does it matter?" His voice was low, not weary, but coiled. Then the refrigerator door slammed shut. The echo rolled through the house like a gunshot muffled in velvet. "I told you this project is demanding. You wouldn't understand."

She studied him. He looked wrong. Not just tired... hollowed. There was a feverish gleam beneath the exhaustion, a hunger that didn't belong to work or ambition. His pupils were wide. His breath too shallow.

"Aubrey," she said softly, "are you all right? You're... not looking so well."

He turned toward her. The smile he gave not unkind but empty. "I don't have time for this," he said. He brushed past her. The movement was abrupt, and she caught a faint chemical smell, disinfectant and something sharp, metallic, like ozone after lightning. "If you need someone to talk to about your feelings, call your friend James. He seems happy to listen."

Her body went cold. "What? What did you say?"

113

He stopped halfway through the doorway. He glanced back over his shoulder. The overhead light caught his features in stark relief, the hollow of his cheeks, the tautness of his jaw. A smile flickered and died.

"You think I don't know?" It wasn't jealousy in his tone. Impossible. He wasn't jealous. He was the opposite of jealous. He didn't care, so long as it didn't affect him. His gaze was dissection, cold, deliberate cruelty offered with a surgeon's precision. "What are you doing with him instead of making this place a home?"

"What are you doing instead of making a home with me?" She threw back.

"Don't change the subject."

"Don't attack me." She defended herself.

"You attack me for my lovers. What about you?"

"If I had one, I could see your reaction."

"Oh, that's right. Like anyone would fuck you."

"You don't have to be cruel, Aubrey," she whispered. But she knew better. She simply said, "Gaslighting."

"Cruel?" His mouth twisted. He ignored her statement. "I'm not the one playing house with the neighbor while pretending this place isn't rotting around us."

"This house is rotting because of you!" she snapped, the words too loud, too hot. "You brought us here with your promises and your projects, and all you've done since is hide at work. You haven't even looked at the first round of renovation."

For a heartbeat, something shifted behind his eyes, surprise, maybe, or regret. Then it vanished. His expression flattened. "You think you know what's going on?" he said. His voice was quieter, the danger in it more intimate. "You don't. You never have."

Her pulse roared in her ears. "So, what's so damned difficult."

His jaw tightened. He looked at her. Even she noticed, for the first time, he saw her not as his wife, but as an obstacle. His gaze was feverish, unblinking. "I'm accomplishing things you could never comprehend."

"No, I don't think so. I think you're attempting to accomplish something but haven't yet, other than having an affair. *Stereotypical* men have had mistresses for millennia, hon." She threw back.

He cringed when she said it. She almost smirked but didn't want him to see. He said, "You have no idea how important our research is. If you did, things would be different."

"Hmmm." She rolled her eyes, "Yes, I'm sure the world is just waiting for your research on how to maintain a double life."

"Will you stop that? So, what? We haven't been a couple for years."

"Will *you* stop that?" She cocked an eyebrow. "You are the liar and the fraud when it comes to relationships. Why the hell should I believe anything you say about your *important* work. Wining and dining a side piece doesn't qualify as important work."

He winced again, but she ignored it. "It was your responsibility to get a *divorce* when you decided you didn't want to 'be a couple'. Not string me along for years. I can't imagine what kind of deception you bring professionally if the trainwreck of your personal life is any indication. I'm sure your research is just as fraudulent and deceptive."

The words landed with a weight she didn't expect. Not evasive... absolute. He turned, glared at her, and went up the stairs. "I'm going to bed," he said without looking back. The sound of his footsteps faded, slower now, until they blended with the creaks of the house. Then silence.

She stood alone in the kitchen. Her anger had cooled into something denser, heavier, like iron settling in her chest. The light above her flickered once, twice, then steadied. The refrigerator murmured faintly. It was true. There was a chance that his work was absolutely mundane, and he just pretended to give himself importance and disguise his affair. But the paperwork she had proved there was something unusual going on at the Institute.

She heard the faint tick of the old wall clock, and beneath that, something else, a low rumble, like a faraway machine behind the walls. The house was listening. It always listened.

She crossed to the study. Her movements automatic. She pulled out the envelope of newspaper clippings and documents from the attic. She spread them across the table. The papers whispered against the wood. Dry, papery breaths, that curled at the corners.

The faint smell of mildew rose up, mingled with dust and something sharper: burnt paper, or hair singed by fire. Her eyes found the photograph again.

Dr. Reyland Hayes

The name printed below the image was smudged, but the face was clear, hollow cheeks. That same penetrating stare. For a moment, she saw Aubrey superimposed over it. The resemblance so exact it made her skin crawl. The thought arrived uninvited and terrible in its simplicity:

What if it wasn't resemblance?

What if it was *inheritance*? The air tightened around her. It pressed close, until the silence broke. A faint laugh came from somewhere down the hall. A child's laugh. Brief. Bright. Entirely out of place. She spun toward the sound. Nothing there. Just the dim hall, the wallpaper's faint shimmer under the light.

Still, she felt him. Charlie. Watching. Waiting. The temperature dropped just enough for her breath to show. Her fear trembled... then steadied.

"I'll figure it out," she whispered. "I'll make sure he doesn't hurt anyone else."

The laugh faded, not into silence, but into something deeper. The house seemed satisfied. A faint tremor rippled through the floorboards beneath her bare feet, slow, rhythmic,

116

almost like a pulse. She pressed her hand flat against the wall. The quiet held.

She felt it now. The faint, steady heartbeat of the house, patient and alive, echoing her own. And beneath that pulse, a whisper. Not words. Not yet. Just sound. Waiting to become a voice. She wasn't just seeking answers anymore.

She was trespassing into something vast. Something that watched through the walls and remembered every scream, every secret, every experiment. And somewhere below her feet, in the dark belly of the house, Father was awake.

Chapter 23

She couldn't stop thinking of Allura's diary, her grief, her fevered words, the desperation in her handwriting. Her sorrow had seeped through the ink like blood through linen. She felt bound to her. Both had loved men who called their heartlessness "dedication." Both had lived in the same house that whispered back.

Aubrey was unrecognizable. The more she read, the more she saw him in Reyland, obsessed with work, absent even when standing before her. She couldn't believe he hadn't converted part of the home into a laboratory already. Then again, that would have required discretion, hard to manage when you've got a mistress, or a second family, or whatever the hell it was.

He dressed and left by lunch. They didn't speak. She was curious about his strange, seemingly random, visits. *Evidently, he can't decide whether he needs time or not.* She didn't like them. They made her suspicious. Why was he coming home? What did he think he'd find? Would she just explode one day into lunacy and never return? Was he waiting to catch her unraveling, so he could put her away?

The house wasn't quiet after that. One sound seemed to summon the next, the clock striking unevenly, pipes clanging, glass settling in the windowpanes, until the whole atmosphere buzzed with nervous energy. She gathered Allura's papers into a neat bundle and brought them to the study. She'd go through them again soon. Just not yet.

What were the odds her husband would be so much like Allura's? Still, she told herself, Aubrey wouldn't go so far as to experiment on her. That sort of thing couldn't happen today, not with laws, not with oversight. But if he wanted her out of the way, he had other tools. Friends in the medical community. Influence. The ability to have her committed quietly. No one would ever question the respected Dr. Aubrey Bainbridge.

He'd isolated her without even locking a door. It was only lately she'd realized it. He'd tried to become her whole circle, her confidant, her captor. She wondered if it had been deliberate or just the shape their life had taken, piece by piece.

She picked up the duster out of habit and moved from room to room, though she'd cleaned everything the day before. Her hands trembled. The scent of lavender polish and old wood rose like a memory. She finally stepped out into the yard, blinking against the harsh sun.

James was out, as always, trimming hedges that didn't need trimming. When he saw her, he waved, and for a moment, the day felt ordinary. They spoke lightly, neighbors' chatter, nothing important. But her thoughts kept circling the same dark orbit until the words burst from her:

"James, can I ask you something?"

His expression softened. "Of course."

"I'm divorcing Aubrey."

"I gathered as much," he said, not unkindly. "I'm glad you're taking care of yourself. Sorry for what it's cost you."

She hesitated, then went on. "He hasn't gotten the papers. He... accidentally called me last week. I heard him laughing with a woman. They were talking about their plans, one of them was my 'unraveling,' as he put it. James, I think he's going to try and have me committed."

His brow furrowed. "God. You really think he'd do something that cruel?"

"The man I married wouldn't. But that man's been gone for years. I hope it isn't... that I'm wrong. It would be cheaper than divorce, however, and with his network, I'd say he could get just about anything done."

"What do you need me to do?"

"Just keep your eyes open. If I disappear... call my attorney. And my mother-in-law. Please."

He went pale. "Gabriella... is it really that serious?"

"I hope not. I'd rather be paranoid than right."

They exchanged uneasy smiles, and for a moment she almost felt safe. Until the low growl of an engine reached them.

James turned his head. "Speak of the devil."

Aubrey's Mercedes pulled into the drive, silver and predatory. Her stomach twisted. She sighed. "Again? It's a record. Well. Duty calls."

She walked back to the house, every step heavier than the last. *What the hell? He was just here.* This was indeed strange. Inside, the air was colder. Still. The faint scent of iron threaded through the hall. She called out, "Aubrey?"

He appeared in the kitchen doorway, pale and taut, prominent rings under his eyes. "Where were you?"

"I was outside," she said carefully.

"Outside," he repeated. "With another man."

She was in shock. "Our neighbor?"

He didn't respond, only stared at her, jaw tight, eyes glassy with exhaustion or rage. She had a sudden idea that it was all rehearsed. That he was deliberately looking for things to get angry over. She should've been furious. He was in no position to be jealous.

Instead, a strange laughter bubbled up from her chest, light and brittle. "You think I'm having an *affair*?" She giggled again, sharper this time. "That's rich, Aubrey. How many women have *you* taken to hotels? To conferences? And I speak to a neighbor... suddenly it's treason."

He glared, lips trembling. "I don't know what you're talking about."

"Sure you don't. Sure, sure.... You've been faithful to your one true love. Yourself."

"Don't talk to me like that." His face twisted into something she didn't recognize, something thinner, colder.

"No?" she said softly. "Remember... I have photographs."

The words landed like a blow. He froze. The blood drained from his face.

"Photographs?" he repeated.

"Yes, Aubrey. Photographs. And *witnesses.* And receipts. Used tickets..." She almost divulged she had lab notes and documents. She bit her tongue to keep that one quiet.

True, she didn't have witnesses, but she did have everything else. Someone witnessed it to take said photographs. He didn't speak again. He simply turned, retrieved his keys, and left. The door shut quietly behind him, but the silence that followed was deep, thick, alive.

She stood for a long time. She just listened to the car fade into the distance. The house creaked. Somewhere deep inside the walls, something seemed to sigh with her. *Well, that was that.*

She wandered to the study. She needed distraction. The scent of dust and paper steadied her. She opened Allura's bundle again. A yellowed clipping slid free, a boy's photograph. *Charlie Hayes, age 8. Died of fever in his father's hospital.* The article was brief, sterile.

There were loose pages beneath it, and one more diary entry, the last one.

July 25th, 1925

Reyland put me in his clinic. I know I'll never leave. Maybe it's for the best. I don't want to live without Charlie. I think Reyland means to marry his nurse. I saw them in the corridor, her back against the wall, his hands under her dress. I should have been angry. I felt nothing.

She only came here because I felt sorry for her. He first said she was unfit for the hospital. But now she's part of his "plans."

I don't know what he's done, but I keep growing weaker. Something is wrong. This is not the flu. The air whispers. I see things. The

same lights Charlie saw. They're waiting for me too.

She pressed her palm against the paper. For a moment, she felt the heat of Allura's fever. The words seemed to tremble under her touch. She was grateful that, at least, Aubrey couldn't lock her away so easily. She hoped.

The phone rang. She jumped. "Hello?"

"Gabriella," Aubrey said.

Her breath hitched. "Aubrey? What's going on? You just left. Are you all right?"

"Never better," he said, but his voice sounded wrong, hollow, like he was speaking from another room, another time.

"What do you want?"

"What were you doing?"

"Reading," she answered.

"That's good," he murmured. "Reading keeps the mind open."

She frowned. It was her husband... but it wasn't. "Ok. So I'm going to get back to it, I'll—"

"Do you feel them watching you?"

Her blood ran cold. "What?"

"The shadows," he said softly. "They're watching you."

She stood frozen. "What the hell, Aubrey?"

He chuckled faintly. "I'm kidding, Gabby. God, take a joke."

Her hand shook. "Why would you even say that?"

"Did I?" His tone shifted, confused. "I said the neighbors are watching. You misheard me."

"No, you didn't."

"Calm down. You're overworked again."

"Stop talking to me like I'm sick."

"Don't worry," he said. "Father is with you. He'll keep you safe."

The line went dead.

The lights flickered once. Then again. The air thickened, heavy and buzzing, like static. From the corner of her vision, something darker began to move. It rose from the foot of the sofa, long, deliberate, human shaped. She couldn't move, couldn't breathe, couldn't even scream. The house exhaled. And she finally understood what Allura meant by *the lights behind the ceiling boards.*

The air around her rippled. It pressed down heavy and cold. The shadow stretched taller. Its edges quivered like smoke struggling to stay solid. Her eyes watered from something like frigid pressure. It wasn't just dark, it was alive. It leaned, it swayed, as though listening. When it moved, the boards beneath the floor gave a tremendous cracking.

She fell back onto the oversized ottoman. The floor had to be caving in. Something brushed her ankle. Not warm. Not cold. Just *present.*

Her pulse hammered. Every instinct screamed to move, to *run,* but her body betrayed her. The house groaned again, timbers flexing, as though the thing inside the walls was drawing a breath it hadn't taken in years.

The nearby lamp flickered once more, then steadied, its light dimming to the color of bone. A shadow formed, a faint outline of a man, shoulders narrow, head bowed.

"Father," it said. The word was soundless, shaped in the air itself, trembling through her chest.

Her heart lurched. "No," she mouthed, but no sound came.

The thing tilted its head, curious. Its face, if it had one, was a shifting hollow. Within it pulsed the faintest light, white and slow, like the flicker behind the ceiling boards.

Her breath came in shallow gasps. The air stank of ozone and iron. The walls shivered as though struck by distant thunder. The force held her down. She struggled and tried to jerk from its grasp, but she couldn't move. It didn't seem to be touching her at all, but her body froze.

Then came the humming, soft at first, then swelling. It was an all-too-familiar melody. Aubrey's tune. The one he used to hum absentmindedly when he studied.

Her paralysis broke like glass. She lunged for the lamp, knocking it sideways. The room vanished into black. The song followed. It was right behind her ear now.

She turned. The shadow was gone. Only the smell remained, iron and wax and something faintly sweet, like a spent bouquet.

She stumbled from the living room. She was shaking, half-blind, until her hand found the wall. The boards were trembling. Faint light leaked from between them, white iridescent veins threading through wood. They pulsed once. Twice. Then stilled.

She sank to the floor when she reached the front door. She couldn't run outside in her state. She curled up into a ball and waited. The shadow had been right behind her. It was gone now.

The attic above gave one long, hollow creak, like a door opening. And somewhere in the dark, the man's voice whispered, **"Do you see them yet?"**

Chapter 24

Morning crept in pale and uncertain, the light thin as gauze and too weak to reach the corners of the house. Sleep never really came. The echo of that shadow, *"Do you see it yet?"* It kept turning through her mind like a moth flittering at glass.

The house carried a strange rhythm. Each room felt tilted, slightly rearranged. As though someone wandered through while she slept and nudged everything just enough to disturb the balance. Nothing *looked* wrong, yet everything felt wrong.

She crossed the landing on her way down. The wallpaper along the staircase rippled in uneven bubbles, cool beneath her fingertips. A damp chill filled the air. When she pressed her finger to the wall, the moisture smeared red. The faded roses of the pattern seemed to bleed into her skin. A smell lingered, faint and musty.

In the kitchen, she scrubbed her hand under the tap until the water ran clear. The chill of it bit at her knuckles. The pipes groaned beneath the floor, their echo hollow and deep.

Her phone buzzed on the counter, sharp and sudden in the quiet. Francis. She hesitated before answering. "Francis?"

"Gabby?" The older woman's voice rushed through the speaker, brittle and uneven, like wind through dead leaves.

"It's good to hear from you," she said, grateful that someone in the outside world thought of her. "Is everything all right?"

A pause stretched between them. A faint clock ticked somewhere on the other end.

"I don't know," Francis said at last. "Aubrey came by yesterday. He wouldn't say much, only that he was close to something important. But he looked strange. Not just tired. His eyes had a strange shine to them, like he was hiding something."

She leaned against the counter. The tile felt cold through her robe. "He looks strange," she said softly. "But, he hasn't spent any real time here in weeks. He'll come home every few days for fresh clothes and maybe to sleep a couple of hours. Unless it is to find something to be angry over."

"I was afraid of that." Francis drew a breath. "Gabby, I think he's doing something he shouldn't. I have the worst feelings lately."

"So do I." The words slipped out before she could stop them. Her voice sounded smaller than she meant it to. She should've kept her mouth shut.

The sound of her name in Francis's mouth, that gentle *Gabby*, tugged something inside her chest. The silence that followed was thick, broken only by the steady drip of the faucet.

"I worry about you," Francis said. Her voice sounded thin and far away, as though it traveled through fog. "I didn't realize how far Aubrey had gone. He's so much like his father. I had such hope he would break that cycle. That there would finally be a good Bainbridge man."

A pause followed. The sound of her breath trembled through the receiver. "I'm sorry," she said. "I wish it could have been different."

"Don't apologize," she murmured. "You've been wonderful. Truly. We'll get through this and visit the spa together."

Francis's tone softened. "You've been a perfectly lovely daughter-in-law. I was hesitant when he first married you, but that's to be expected. You never caused a scandal or gave anyone a reason to gossip. You've proven your grace and your place."

She heard the faint sound of a sniffle. The rustle of fabric. "Anyway," Francis said. "I shouldn't carry on. Just be careful."

"Of course. You too."

Her gaze lifted toward the ceiling. The faintest draft stirred the air above her. She imagined the house like a sleeping animal, breathing in slow rhythm.

126

Francis's voice cut through the quiet. "I think he's pulling you into something awful. You need to be careful."

"I am."

"No," Francis said softly. "You believe you are, but I don't think any of us can ever be careful enough."

The line crackled. A hiss rose between them. Then something shifted on the call, a sound too low to be static. A breath. A whisper. Male. *He is already inside.* The connection went dead.

"Francis?" She broke the silence. Nothing answered. Only the hollow click of the line.

Chapter 25

The days remained rainy and overcast. The house had proved to be remarkably resilient with the harsh weather. She toyed with ideas for the next phase of renovations. The shadow had not returned but she often felt it near.

The front door opened. The sound slid through the house like a blade through silk. His footsteps followed, measured, deliberate. They moved across the floorboards in a rhythm she had once known too well. Each step carried ownership, not hesitation.

She remained still in the kitchen, one hand braced on the counter, her pulse thick and slow in her throat. The refrigerator hummed behind her, soft and steady, the only sound that dared exist between them.

"Gabriella?"

His voice floated from the foyer, calm but cold.

She turned. Aubrey stood there, his hair damp, his clothes smelling faintly of rain and antiseptic. The redness at the edges of his eyes might have looked like fatigue to anyone else. She saw calculation. The small curl of his mouth reached for warmth but never found it.

"Why are you here? Again?" Her voice came quieter than she intended. "I thought you needed time."

"I was worried," he said. His words came smooth, polished, too even. "You sounded shaken last night."

Her stomach tightened until it felt hollow. "Last night?"

"Last night." He spoke easily, as if recalling something harmless. "You said the lights were flickering. You thought someone was in the house. I came to check on you."

Her breath caught. The hum of the refrigerator filled the silence. "I never texted you."

He frowned with practiced restraint. The expression she used to mistake for patience. "Gabby, you're exhausted. I texted around eleven to see how you were. That's all. You didn't answer."

The room seemed to contract. The air thickened, too still, too warm. "I didn't text at all," she said. "I certainly didn't tell you about lights or that I was afraid."

He smiled, barely. "Yes, you did." He gave an exaggerated sigh, "I worry about you, Gabby." His voice softened, feigned sympathy creeping into the edges. "Should I stay here? Take care of you?"

"Stop it, Aubrey." Her throat felt raw. "You're not going to do that again."

He blinked slowly, tilting his head as if her defiance confused him. "What do you mean?"

She studied him, her heartbeat steady, no longer frantic but deliberate. The light above them buzzed faintly, casting a thin sheen over the damp on his collar. "Are you sure *you're* well, Aubrey?"

"Of course." His tone rose with that familiar, brittle confidence. The same voice he used in arguments, in lies, in research notes written over nights she hadn't been allowed to question.

She stepped closer, close enough to catch the faint, metallic scent that clung to his coat. "Are you absolutely certain?" He didn't answer. The silence between them deepened, thick and waiting.

"Of course, Gabby. Why?" His tone dripped with something sticky and artificial. Every word stretched and softened until it felt like mockery. He had never spoken that way to her before. The sound slid over her skin, cold and false.

She drew in a long, steady breath. The air in the kitchen tasted of copper and dust. "Through fifteen years, I have had pneumonia, sinus infections, the flu, food poisoning, and strep

129

throat. Not once did you take care of me. I have sat through power outages and nights when I thought someone was breaking in. You never cared." The rhythm of her voice cut through the silence, clear and even.

He blinked once, then again, lips parting as if to speak, but no words came. His gaze drifted past her shoulder, toward nothing, searching for something solid to stand on. His mask faltered.

She pressed on before he could rebuild it. "I wouldn't dream of interrupting such important work. I insist you go back and continue." The words landed between them, calm and deliberate.

He shifted back a single step, his balance uncertain. "If you're sure."

"Completely."

Her eyes held his, unflinching. She waited for some small crack to form in his composure. The clock on the counter ticked, sharp and hollow. "The only time you called or texted," she said softly. "Was days ago... on the old line."

"The landline?" He gave a short, humorless laugh. "That thing hasn't worked in years."

"It rang," she repeated.

She crossed the room. The phone hung on the wall, its cord coiled tight. She lifted the receiver. A high, thin whine scraped through the speaker. Then silence.

"Maybe you dreamed it," he said.

He stepped closer. His shoes were silent against the wood. The scent of antiseptic and scorched metal clung to him, sharp and bitter, filling the space between them. Her throat burned when she breathed it in.

"You've been under a lot of stress...." he continued. His voice slow, coaxing. "This house... it gets inside your head. I told you that when we moved in."

Her chest tightened until she could hardly speak. He reached toward her. His fingers hovered inches from her shoulder. She flinched before he touched her. "Don't," she said.

His hand dropped. He had *never* said anything like that before. When they first bought the house, he had mocked the realtor's nervous stories and laughed at the talk of ghosts. He had wanted to turn the place into something sleek and bright, his version of perfection.

His hand fell to his side. The movement quiet and deliberate. The false warmth drained from his voice. It left only something cool and practiced beneath it. "I'll stay a few hours," he said. "Just until you've rested."

He slipped past her. His shoulder brushed the air beside hers, but never actually touched her. The hallway seemed to expand around him. The old floorboards muttered under his weight. Each step carried the same quiet claim, as though the house still knew him.

The air he left behind carried a chemical tang, sharp and sterile. It clung to her skin and filled her lungs until her stomach turned. It was the same smell that came after he was in the lab. Only now, it had a far worse effect on her.

She stood in the kitchen long after he disappeared from sight... listening. The rhythm of his footsteps faded up the staircase, a slow, unhurried ascent that dissolved into the ceiling. Then silence. Thick and unnatural.

Her mind churned. *Why now?* The question pulsed with every heartbeat. He never returned out of concern. He never did anything without reason. He only cared for what could be molded, measured, altered under his gaze. He certainly didn't give two shits for how she felt.

She moved toward the counter with shallow breath. She felt faint. The faint reflection of her face trembled in the steel of the refrigerator. Wide eyes, colorless lips, the ghost of someone trapped inside a life she had built around someone else.

When the last creak of the floor above stilled, she pulled her phone from her pocket. Her fingers slipped once against the smooth glass before finding the right pressure. The screen lit her face in cold blue. The buzz of the wires and the low tick of the pipes steady and close. Somewhere above, a door clicked shut.

She didn't look up. Instead, she gripped the phone tighter and unlocked the screen, her hands trembling against the faint vibration that shivered through the floor beneath her feet.

Recent Calls → Incoming.
No record.

Not a single record. She had no proof of anything. No calls to her cell. She certainly didn't have a record of a call to the landline. In all, she didn't even have a missed notification.

Her thumb scrolled again, desperate for proof. Nothing. The screen glowed faintly in the dim kitchen light, reflecting her face in pale distortion. Only one exchange waited at the bottom, stark and ordinary.

09:02 p.m. —You: Aubrey, the lights keep
flickering and it sounds like someone's trying to
get in downstairs. I'm really scared. Please call.
11:02 p.m. —Aubrey: Are you alright?

Just that simple text, sitting there like an accusation, like a quiet rewrite of history. She knew she didn't send that text. She knew it. But there it was. Dated. Timed. Her pulse climbed. The silence beneath that faint electrical noise felt sentient, waiting.

She stared at the screen until it dimmed to black. Her reflection swallowed in the glass. The house filled the silence with its own noise. A faint vibration rippled through the floorboards, low and rhythmic, like the slow purr of some sleeping creature buried deep beneath her feet.

The air around her pressed close, charged and still. The refrigerator whirred low in the background. Somewhere deep in the walls, something softly clicked. What was happening to her? How could he plant a text like that with the date and time? He wasn't there the night before to orchestrate it.

Her unease was deepened by his presence. Maybe it was his bizarre changes, or maybe the divorce, but she didn't trust him anymore, not even to be in the house. Her gut screamed for her to slip out the back and avoid him at all costs. He wouldn't be here long. She hoped.

She felt like a lab rat watching the scientist manipulate the maze. She couldn't decide how much of the activity she experienced was genuine verses how much he somehow manipulated.

The light above the sink flickered once, then again. Its glow stuttered in the gloom. The noise grew louder. It crawled through the wiring like a heartbeat caught in the walls. Dust loosened from the old plaster and drifted downward in soft, whispering threads that disappeared before reaching the floor.

She looked up. From the narrow seam where ceiling met plaster, a thin line of moisture began to creep downward. It curled like a vein opening beneath the surface. "Well, damn," she whispered. "Did it rupture a line?"

It trailed across the wall in uneven rivulets. The color darkened as it spread, thick and uncertain, more viscous than water should be. The smell reached her before the sight of it settled, iron, salt, and sulfur. Something alive that had begun to rot.

Her nose prickled and her eyes watered. She stepped closer, drawn in spite of herself. The liquid shimmered under the flickering light. It spread across the plaster in delicate streaks that caught the reflection of her face in their sheen. Then, within that thin film of condensation, the movement changed.

Not drips now. Not random patterns. Lines began to form. Each stroke deliberate, trembling, like the script of a hesitant hand. Letters emerged, uncertain and wavering. Words took shape, pulsing faintly as the moisture thickened, as though the house itself wrote to her in its slow, feverish language.

HE'S WATCHING

She gawked. The words on the wall gently rippled and broke apart, dissolving into nothing. The moisture thickened into

133

slow, heavy drips that bled down to the tile floor and into the grout.

The refrigerator gave a sudden shudder. Its motor rattled like something trapped inside it. Every light in the room blinked out. It left her in a thin wash of daylight that slanted through the window. The silence deepened, the air pressed close, charged.

From deep within the walls came a sound. Soft. Human. A sigh that didn't belong to her. She turned toward it, her voice unsteady. "Charlie?"

The answer came in the form of a laugh. It drifted through the stillness, light and small, a child's laugh. Then another voice followed, smooth and deliberate, coiling through the first like a shadow taking form.

"You shouldn't have let him in."

A crack sounded above her, sharp enough to rattle the ceiling light. Her pulse faltered. The door upstairs slammed. The echo rolled through the ceiling like a wave. Footsteps followed, each one slow and deliberate. The boards creaked beneath the weight of someone who knew the layout of her fear.

Then his voice floated down, calm, conversational, so ordinary it made her skin crawl. "Gabriella? The power's out. Must be the wiring."

Her gaze rose to the ceiling. A line of damp plaster pulsed faintly. It swelled and contracted with the rhythm of her heartbeat. "What are you doing?" she whispered.

No reply. Only the slow drip of water, followed by a faint, dragging sound within the wall. A scratch, light and rhythmic, like fingertips brushing from the inside. The lights flared back to life.

Their brilliance came too strong, bleaching the color from the world. The air turned raw with ozone and vibrated against her teeth. In that moment of searing light, she saw him.

At the far end of the hall, a boy stood framed in the glare. His outline flickered, translucent, caught between presence and absence. His head tilted, as though listening to a voice that lived outside of sound. Charlie.

He lifted his hand and pointed upward. The attic door above her opened with a long, aching groan. Dust drifted down like snow. From the darkness beyond came the muted ring of a telephone. The sound warped by time and distance.

The house tilted. She felt it in her feet, in her bones. Every board, every nail, every inch of plaster moved in quiet harmony with her pulse, as though it waited for her next heartbeat to decide what it would do. The water break she'd witnessed earlier was gone. The wall was dry.

Minutes slipped by, or perhaps hours. Time thinned until it lost its edge. When the front door finally shut, the sound came soft and deliberate. His footsteps faded down the walk. Then nothing. Only the slow, uneven rhythm of her own breathing filled the space he left behind. His car came to life and drove off in the distance.

She climbed the stairs once the silence settled. Her hand brushed the wall. Her fingertips glided over cool plaster that seemed to thrum beneath her touch. The pulse felt faint but alive, as though the house claimed her heartbeat for its own.

She checked the bedroom first. The air smelled faintly of starch and linen, with an undercurrent of something metallic. The drawers sat closed. The bed remained neat, the sheets untouched. No sign of life. No sign of him.

One room at a time, she moved through the house. Each space seemed to gently slant when she entered. A whisper in the curtains, a soft pop in the floorboards beneath her weight. Nothing had been taken. Nothing disturbed, yet the stillness felt staged, too deliberate, as if the house decided what she was meant to see.

She went to the attic next. She grasped the cord for the light. The bulb flickered, then steadied into a dim yellow glow that spread thinly across the rafters.

Dust drifted down in slow spirals, soft and shimmering in the beam. The air carried the dry scent of old timber and insulation, laced with something faintly sweet, like wilted flowers.

She turned slowly, her eyes scanned the clutter, the trunks, the old furniture, the covered mirrors. Everything rested in the same position as before, yet she could not shake the feeling of eyes behind her. The antique light hissed faintly. Beneath that susurration, a deeper rumble moved through the floorboards, quiet but constant.

Aubrey might've intended for her to unravel, but he was slipping. She felt it in every word he spoke, every silence he left behind. Whether his mind had fractured or he planned to unravel from the start, she refused to be the one to come apart. Her pulse steadied. Her breath grew even.

The strange calls had not come from the lab. They had come from here. From the walls. From the house that had learned her name and borrowed her husband's voice.

Whatever lingered within its bones, whatever had spoken through him, had claimed him completely. And it waited now, patient and listening, to see if she would follow.

Chapter 26

She stared at the teacup in her hands. The porcelain quivered beneath her touch, delicate as bone. Each tremor sent the rim clinking against the saucer, a brittle, rhythmic sound that fractured the quiet. Her fingers ached with the effort to steady them. She set the cup down; afraid she would drop it.

Francis's voice echoed through her mind, soft yet unyielding.

Project *EIDOLON*.

Even the name seemed to sink in her chest. The hollow resonance spread through her ribs and lingered, heavy as a tolling death bell.

The tea had gone cold. The residue caught her reflection in distorted fragments, eyes dark, face pale, mouth set in silence. She should have been undone by what she'd heard: the deception, the calculated cruelty he cloaked behind locked doors and midnight returns. Yet her grief had sharpened. The shock had burned clean and left only the hard clarity of rage.

For years, she worked to patch the life he had so persistently unraveled. She bent herself smaller, softened each edge, convinced herself that his distance reflected her failings. Her loneliness. Her need. Her lack. But the truth stood unblinking now. Aubrey had not drifted. He had chosen. He had turned toward something darker and left her chained in the shadow of his ambition.

Francis reached across the table for her. The faint tremor in her hand betrayed both age and urgency. Her voice came low, threaded with a tenderness that made Gabriella's chest ache. "You're stronger than you realize," she said. "Don't let him convince you otherwise."

She nodded, though her throat felt too tight to speak. She rose carefully, smoothing her coat though the fabric clung unevenly to her damp palms. "Thank you... for everything."

Francis's eyes softened. For a moment, all the steel in her expression gave way to something maternal, fragile, almost fearful. "Be careful, dear," she murmured. "Don't let him use his memory against you. He isn't who he was."

Outside, the air pressed cool and wet against her face. The scent of rain mingled with smoke from a distant chimney, earthy and old. The words followed her into the gray afternoon, quiet as breath but heavy enough to weigh down her steps.

Later that evening, as the last threads of light drained from the sky, her phone rang. The sound tore through the stillness, sharp and sudden. She reached for it slowly, her hand trembled before she touched the receiver.

The voice on the other end spoke with professional calm, distant but heavy with meaning. Someone from the hospital. A neighbor had found Francis collapsed in her foyer. Cardiac failure, they said. Sudden. Unpredictable. It caused her to fall down the stairs.

The words slipped through the line with the precision of a diagnosis and the weight of finality. Her knees weakened. She lowered herself into the nearest chair. The wood creaked beneath her, the air in the room too thin to hold a breath. The silence that followed felt immense, like sound itself had fled.

Had Francis known her end was near? Was that the reason she became so attentive and affectionate? Her mind raced through all the things she could've done to prevent it. Maybe she should have agreed to stay with Francis when she offered. Maybe the guilt and grief from her son's proclivities pushed her over the edge.

There were hundreds of things she could've done differently. Maybe she should've lived with her. Guarded her. Maybe that would've bought her a little more time.

The countless questions and bargaining clouded her mind. She almost didn't notice the house. In the walls, the pipes ticked. The slow, uneven rhythm of metal expanding and cooling. Each pop echoed faintly through the floorboards and mimicked a fading heartbeat.

The hospital had tried to reach Aubrey. For hours, the nurse said. Always the same result. No answer. No voicemail. Only silence.

He never answered when it mattered. That didn't surprise her at all. Since she was still next of kin, the duty fell to her. She sat at the kitchen table, the phone cradled in her hand, the surface cool against her skin. Outside, twilight pooled against the windows. Her reflection was a dim blur in the glass.

She didn't want to grieve with him. She did not even want to hear his voice. Aubrey had unsettled her since the move, especially when he grew distant again. And now, the thought of speaking to him filled her with a quiet dread.

The nurse's voice still lingered in her mind long after the call ended. There had been something beneath her careful tone, a pause too long to be polite, a hesitation that said more than words could.

In that pause, she felt it. The pressure around her throat, cold and invisible. The faint sense of being watched from a great distance. They knew something. Or suspected it. She stared at the dark window. The reflection of her empty chair stared back.

Poor Francis. If only they had connected sooner. Before Aubrey's control had drawn such clean lines between them. Before the house, before the secrets, before all of it. If only she had seen him clearly. But *if onlys* didn't matter anymore. The pipes whispered again, faint and rhythmic, as the last light left the room.

She took a deep breath and resumed the chore of calling him. Once. Twice. Six times. Each attempt rang into nothing. The hollow sound of distance swallowing her voice. On the seventh, when she had stopped counting the rings, he finally answered.

"Aubrey," she said. The name came out uneven. She swallowed and tried again, forcing her tone to steady. She bit her lip to stay focused. "I... I have awful news."

"What?" His voice was flat but edged with irritation. No curiosity. No alarm. Only the weary cadence of someone interrupted at an inconvenient moment.

Her fingers tightened around the phone until her knuckles whitened. "Francis is dead."

The silence that followed felt alive. She didn't imagine quiet. She figured he'd be angry, accusatory, despondent, anything but what he was. She could hear the hum of the line, the faint hiss of static, her own breath. But not his. Not a gasp, not a word. Then, at last, he spoke.

"That's unfortunate."

The words landed without weight, without emotion. A soft clicking followed, sharp, rhythmic, deliberate. It sounded like fingernails tapping against glass.

"Unfortunate? *Unfortunate?*" Her voice cracked, too loud in the stillness. "Are you a robot? She was your *mother.*"

He said nothing. Only the roar of silence filled the space between them, steady and calm. It was a mechanical imitation of life.

"She was under a lot of stress," he said after a long pause, his tone light, detached. "She always worried too much about things that didn't concern her."

She pressed the phone tighter to her ear. Her stomach tightened until she thought she might be sick. "She was your mother...." she said again, almost pleading. This can't be his reaction.

The line crackled softly. A whisper of electricity bled through the silence. Then his breath shifted, closer now, intimate, as if he were speaking beside her rather than through the phone.

"You're overwrought again, Gabriella," he murmured. "I do worry about you. But I'm busy here. I only answered because I thought you might be upset."

No. Something wasn't right. She drew the phone away and stared at the screen. The timer sat at zero. The call had not connected.

When she lifted it again, the voice that spoke was not the same. It had slowed, deepened, thick with something heavy that crawled beneath her skin.

"Has Father spoken to you yet?"

Her body went cold. The phone slipped through her fingers. It clattered against the table before it rolled to the floor. The sound seemed to echo too long, as though the room itself had leaned in to listen.

For a moment, she could not move. The air felt syrupy, thick. When she finally bent to pick up the phone, its screen remained dark.

She unlocked it with shaking hands and opened her call history. Nothing. No outgoing calls. No voicemail. Only one missed call from a blocked number, time stamped two minutes before she had tried to reach him. No, she wasn't trying to reach him again. She sent a text that said it was urgent he call. Something had happened to his mother. He could call this time.

Her pulse thudded in her ears. The overhead light flickered once, twice, then steadied, buzzing faintly. The glow it cast seemed thinner than before, as if the room itself had grown hollow.

She stared at the phone. Her reflection trembled across the black glass. The air smelled faintly of ozone and old paper. Somewhere behind the walls, the faintest vibration moved, steady, rhythmic, familiar. She knew the house listened. She texted Aubrey to call her because it was urgent.

Sleep never came. The dark stretched on without shape. An oppressive silence that sang, just beneath hearing. She tried to read, but the words refused to stay still. They slid across the page. They slipped from her grasp like water through her hands.

The din in the walls grew stronger. At first, it pulsed like a faint murmur of plumbing, harmless and distant. It then deepened, slow and rhythmic, like a tribal drumbeat beneath the floorboards. It crept up through the frame of the house, through the bedposts, through her ribs, until her pulse fell into sync with it. The house was awake.

She felt it waking, slow and patient. The air changed with each inhale. The walls expanded and contracted with her, as though it had learned her rhythm. Every noise became a syllable. The vowels of settling wood, the consonants of the hissing radiator, and the faint zephyr of her breath.

Chapter 27

She rose and crossed to the desk around midnight. Insomnia arose again. The floor was colder than it should have been. The boards were slightly damp beneath her bare feet, like a fog hovered above the hardwood.

Aubrey eventually texted back and said he already knew about Francis. He would handle the arrangements. His words were brief. Cold. Final.

She could see him reacting like that if she died. She was an unwanted spouse, tolerated because she kept the house clean and the laundry fresh. A utilitarian accessory for practical liaisons with the outside world, when needed.

She couldn't see that reaction from his mother's passing. That was a whole new diabolical level, even for him. Each day made her realize she knew him less and less. Francis had been cold, but there was never a question of her love or care for him.

She couldn't think of it. She would drive herself crazy. She reached for the folder of Bainbridge family records. It was meant for the bedroom bookshelf. She had put it away months earlier to protect it while the room was repainted. Back when she still believed they would have a family. Aubrey's father gave him a copy when he turned 18 so he would have 'his lineage with him wherever he went'. She never got around to reading it.

The neglect was obvious. The folder exhaled a cloud of dust as she opened it. The air smelled of old paper. She coughed. She brushed her fingertips along the top page, the texture dry and brittle, edges curled like burnt leaves.

A single sheet from the back of the file slipped loose and drifted toward the floor. It landed soundlessly, face down. She knelt and grabbed it.

The parchment was rough against her skin, thick and uneven, as though it had been handmade. The ink had bled slightly, spreading into the fibers. The handwriting remained deliberate, elegant, each curve dark and certain. At the top, one name stood clear, stark against the yellowed paper, as if it had been written yesterday.

The Bainbridge Trust, 1941.

Transfer of Title – Hayes Estate

The truth cut through her like a shard of ice. He didn't *stumble* upon the house. They owned it, held it, buried their secrets inside it. He had not discovered the house. He had come home to it.

How could anything he did shock her? She shouldn't be as surprised as she was. It was all a lie. Everything. Her stomach twisted so tightly she thought she would be sick.

The floor beneath her feet vibrated with a deep, subterranean groan. A kind of sound that didn't belong to wood or earth but to something older, something waking. The lamp on the desk flickered once, twice, then went dark with a muted pop. The air filled with the scorched scent of burnt dust and hot metal.

Then came the sound. *Tch. Tch. Tch.* Soft, measured, deliberate. She stood, her breath shallow. The tapping drew her upward. Each step she took on the staircase creaked. The boards bent beneath her soles like leather stretched too thin. She struggled to maintain her balance.

The air on the second floor hung heavy with moisture. The walls exhaled the odor of mildew and rot. The slow decay of old paint and older paper. The tapping led her to the same guest bedroom. The one that always felt colder than the rest. The door stood ajar. Its edge brushed against the frame with a faint whine when she pushed it open.

The room appeared still, untouched. Yet the air carried a charge that prickled her skin. Dust drifted in the light like pale ash. She turned slowly, and her eyes found the mirror. That same creepy mirror that Charlie and Father appeared in.

The reflection rippled. The smooth surface swam as if stirred by invisible hands. Liquid shadows twisted beneath the glass. Dark shapes took form, elongated, human, but wrong. One figure leaned forward, its face hidden, and pressed a palm against the other side. The mirror shuddered, bending inward as if it might split.

She stepped back, her voice a whisper. "Stop." The shape tilted its head. The gesture looked almost gentle, but something in it felt cruel. Its mouth moved, silent, deliberate. The air grew tight.

Pressure crushed her chest. Her ribs strained. Her throat closed against the weight. She fell to her knees. Her hands clawed for breath. The world narrowed to a smear of color and motion.

"Stop," she gasped. The word barely escaped her lips.

The weight lifted. The mirror stilled. Only her reflection stared back. White skin, shaking hands, wide eyes that didn't really resemble her own. A rumble came overhead. It sounded like the roof was falling in.

She stumbled into the hall. The air was too thick. Each breath scraped through her lungs. A sound cracked above her, deep and long, like timber breaking under an impossible strain. She wondered if the roof was collapsing. Tiny tendrils of dust fell from the ceiling.

As she regained her breath, she glanced toward the attic door. It hung open. The black void beyond it yawning. She had closed it earlier. She was certain she had.

Still, she climbed. Each step moaned beneath her, the rhythm echoed up through the narrow stairwell. The air grew colder with every movement. When she reached the top, the chill met her like a living thing, sharp and wet. It sank through her clothes into her bones.

The silence carried weight, deep and watching. She looked back. Father was near. She felt his shadow, the one that held her down, somewhere close.

The attic held the dry scent of time. Dust thickened the air, soft as ash, and beneath it drifted another odor, metallic, unmistakable, like the ghost of rust or blood. Her flashlight swept across the rafters. Something shifted in there. The light caught the silvered edges of cobwebs and the faint shimmer of drifting particles.

On the far wall, a new crack traced downward through the old plaster. As she stared, it spread, slow and deliberate, widening with the sound of falling rocks. Dust poured from it in a veil, glowing in the pale light.

She stepped closer. The floor shifted with a low moan. The crack deepened, widening until she could see the dark cavity within. Something pale reflected the light. Smooth. Curved.

Bone.

She held her breath. She inched nearer. Each movement careful. Her hand trembled as she angled the light. More pale shapes emerged in that darkness. Ribs. Skulls. A lattice of remains packed tight together. Dozens. Perhaps hundreds. They fused into the brick and the splintered beams as though the house itself had digested them or grown around them.

The smell grew thick, dry air heavy with the sweetness of rot and the sharp sting of copper. The light quivered in her hand.

She tried to see farther into the void. Some skulls appeared to grin through cracked teeth; others seemed frozen mid-scream. A few were heartbreakingly small.

Her body jerked backward as she suffered another fit of coughing. Air rasped through her throat in short, uneven pulls. The silence around her felt alive, pressing hard enough against her eardrums that they clicked in protest. Then, beneath that suffocating stillness, a whisper rose.

"You found us." The voice carried no direction. It slithered through the air like breath on cold glass. The lightbulb overhead sputtered. It cast the attic in a broken rhythm of light

and shadow. Each flash distorted the walls, and made the bones appear to twitch.

The floor trembled once beneath her feet, just enough to rattle the loose boards. A chill traced the length of her spine. Then, abruptly, the light steadied.

She returned down the steps. Each step pounded on the stairs. Every impact sent shudders through the frame of the house. The air filled with the scent of dust and iron. She couldn't escape it. She tasted it as she gasped, her tongue coated in grit.

Behind her, the darkness followed, stretching, breathing. She felt the skulls watching. Their presence pressed at her back, cold and patient. The weight of centuries crowded the narrow hall. Doors closed as she passed. It sounded like every light bulb exploded as they closed.

She did not need to ask how long the bones had been there. Too long. And now, they had begun to wake.

Chapter 28

She called the police as soon as she could form words again. The dispatcher's voice was polite but distracted, her questions perfunctory. Apparently human remains inside a wall were not the strangest thing she'd heard all week. Or maybe they didn't believe her.

The officer moved through the house with quiet disbelief. He didn't seem to believe the remains were going to be human. Until he saw them. His flashlight trembled slightly in his gloved hand. He didn't linger long in the attic. One look at the bones drained the color from his face.

He cleared his throat, and said they had been there many decades, but not to disturb them. He would return with a forensic team as soon as they were available. He left without another glance at her. He seemed unnerved by something other than the bodies. She could imagine. He probably saw the shadows closing in.

She thought about packing a bag, about leaving, even for a night. There were hotels nearby, rooms with clean sheets and impersonal lamps and walls that did not whisper. But the idea felt absurd. She had lived here for months, eating breakfast below the bones of the forgotten. What was the point of going elsewhere? They weren't going anywhere.

The house had gone still again. Not exactly peaceful, never that, but heavy with anticipation, as though it waited for something to happen. Each sound echoed too long in the silence: the creak of a chair, the sigh of the refrigerator, the faint tick of the cooling pipes beneath the floor.

She tried reaching Aubrey again. She didn't know if she were legally obligated to tell him about the bones or not, but he was currently the home's owner, too. It probably wouldn't matter to him. Message after message went unanswered. His reply came hours later, a text with only two words.

I know.

Nothing else. No question, no condolence, no trace of grief. He was as apathetic for the deceased upstairs as he was for his own mother. The police called her that afternoon but didn't mention the remains. They simply stated Francis's death would be listed as natural until the autopsy came back.

The mail came at lunchtime and with it the moment she'd been dreading. She sat at the kitchen table, the envelope from her attorney rested before her. She slid a fingertip along the edge of the open flap, tracing its neat precision. The documents inside were stacked in perfect order, every signature in place. The paper inside smelled faintly of ink and toner, sharp and clean against the air gone stale.

Divorce papers.

The ink gleamed faintly in the afternoon light, a blue sheen like a vein beneath skin. The pages lay motionless, final, silent.

Her reflection wavered in the polished surface of the table. Pale face, hollow eyes, the ghost of someone who had forgotten what peace was like. What simplicity was like. What blessed ignorant bliss was like.

Outside, wind moved through the trees, soft but insistent. It had been so long since she'd seen a full sunny day. Now the sun seemed like a fair-weather friend. The branches brushed against the siding, whispering along the walls.

The sound might have been nothing more than weather. Or the house reminding her that it was still listening. She looked down at the papers.

Summons and Petition for Divorce..

She stared at the signature for a long time, her pulse rose in slow disbelief. The handwriting belonged to her, every loop, every curl exactly, but she had no memory of signing the papers. The penmanship looked confident, almost graceful, as though the hand that had written it hadn't trembled the way hers did now.

Unraveling.

She called her attorney. The phone felt slick against her palm. The man's voice came on, calm and clipped, his tone too polished, too rehearsed.

"You were confident in your decision, Gabriella," he said. "Is there a problem?"

"I... I don't remember signing these exact papers," she replied. The words came thin, almost fragile. "How long ago did I—"

He gave a short, patient chuckle. "You must be exhausted. It was quick, yes, but you seemed certain. It's all filed properly."

Her throat tightened. The walls creaked softly behind her, boards shifting in a rhythm that sounded almost deliberate. Listening. Waiting.

She forced a laugh, light and brittle. "No problem," she said. "It just happened so much faster than I expected. I guess Francis's death hit harder than I thought."

"Sure," he replied. "I am so sorry to hear about it."

They finished their call. She set the phone down slowly. Her fingers trembled against the table. The stillness in the house thickened until even her breath seemed to echo.

Then her phone rang again. Aubrey. The sound split the air, sharp and shrill. She knew it was coming. She hesitated, then answered.

"Divorce?" His voice carried no greeting, no preamble, just the word, sharp and precise. Bizarrely, he was far more emotional over the divorce than his mother's death. He asked, "Seriously?"

Her breath stuttered. "Aubrey. It all moved so fast, now Francis is gone—"

"Whatever," he interrupted. He didn't even listen. "Why don't you tell me what this is actually about?" He said it like she was a child pulling a stunt.

"What isn't it about?" She fought to steady her tone. "The lies. The secrets. You disappearing... coming home like a stranger. Acting like I'm the one losing my mind. The women. The deception. The years of isolation and neglect. Need I go on?"

A pause stretched thin between them. Then came his answer, flat and cold. "You think you know what I do," he said. "But you don't."

Her fingers dug into the table's edge. "I don't care what you do. I know plenty of doctors with families. Research doctors. Research doctors conducting legitimately important work. They have normal, functioning families. They don't need lies. They don't live double lives."

For a moment, the line went silent except for faint static, breathing, maybe. Then his tone changed. Softer. Silkier. Horrible. "You've made a friend, haven't you?"

The question slid in quietly, casual and wrong. She checked the phone. She was talking to him. Her heart gave a violent kick. "What are you talking about?"

"The neighbor," he said. "Always around. The one you have coffee with."

She pulled the phone from her ear and looked at the screen. The call was still active. Real. Cold spread through her chest. "James? Are you still talking about that?"

"*If* that's his name." His tone sharpened, just enough to try to cut.

"I don't care." She rolled her eyes. It wasn't going to work. "I know you don't know much about how to interact with neighbors, but sometimes you have coffee with them. Sometimes tea. Sometimes, if you're really wild, you'll even have *cake* with them." She smirked. "What the hell are you talking about?" she asked, her voice rose. "You haven't met him. You haven't met anyone here. You never knew any of our neighbors. I hate to break it to you, but I had coffee with the old neighbors, too."

He didn't answer at first. Only the faint hum of the line filled the pause, a quiet static like breathing just behind his words. Then, softly, "You should be more careful who you trust."

Her skin prickled. "What's that supposed to mean? I don't think we're exchanging trade secrets or anything that might cause an international incident."

A low sound came from the other end, something between a laugh and a sigh. "I'm just saying," he murmured, "you've never been a very good judge of character." The line crackled again, then went still. He hung up without another word. The abrupt silence left a hollow ache in her ear.

For a long moment, she sat motionless, the phone still in her hand. He was right about one thing. She was not a good judge of character. She had married him. She had believed every careful lie he'd told, every polished smile, every scientific explanation that neatly erased her instincts.

The quiet that followed didn't feel like peace. It felt alive. The kind of silence that had substance, dense and electric. It unabashedly filled every corner of the room. The lights above the table buzzed, with a thin and insect-like sound. Her phone screen dimmed. The call log blinked to a blank list. No Recent Calls.

Her pulse quickened. The phone felt heavier now, too warm in her hand. It seemed to grow hotter in her hands. She placed it on the table and stepped back.

Another roar came beneath the floor. Subtle, rhythmic, like a breath drawn through the bones of the house. She felt it under her bare feet. The slow vibration that climbed her legs and settled in her chest. What was wrong with her? Maybe the house was haunted, or maybe she was *unraveling*. Was this what unraveling did?

Then she saw it. Through the narrow pane of glass beside the door, something resting on the porch. A padded envelope, beige and unmarked, edges smudged with dirt as though handled by someone who had come straight from the earth. No return address. No postage. Just left there, perfectly centered against the doorframe.

Her breath misted the glass as she leaned closer. The world beyond the porch had gone still. Even the trees had stopped swaying. She opened the door with care, every hinge sighing in protest. The air outside smelled of rain-soaked leaves and the faint metallic tang of soil.

The envelope felt damp when she picked it up. The texture soft and yielding like old paper. She carried it to the table. Her heartbeat thrummed in her fingertips.

The flap tore unevenly. She reached inside and pulled out a manila folder, thick and weighty. Its edges curled from moisture. Across the front, stamped in faded red ink, the letters bled together but still legible:

PROJECT EIDOLON.

The ink looked almost wet, as though it had been marked just moments ago.

PROJECT EIDOLON

PHASE I — NEURO-AFFECTIVE FIELD TESTING / ARCHIVAL COPY

CONFIDENTIAL – EYES ONLY

Her lungs emptied in a single, trembling breath. The edges of her vision pulsed, tightening around the folder like a closing fist. She peeled it open with slow, deliberate care.

Inside lay a stack of papers, photocopied and warped from humidity. Black ink bled through the thin pages, diagrams and graphs layered over lines of typed reports. The smell of old toner and damp paper rose to meet her, acrid, sterile, almost metallic.

She turned the first page.

Dense text filled every inch of it: technical summaries, military references, internal memos. Paragraphs of language stripped of emotion, stripped of humanity. Sentences about dosage rates, neurological interference, behavioral predictability.

Entire sections had been blacked out with thick bands of ink. She flipped to another.

Handwritten notes filled the margins in dark, hurried strokes. The handwriting felt familiar. Angular. Controlled. Aubrey's.

Subject exhibiting improved responsiveness after secondary exposure.

Emotional synchronization effective at ninety-three percent.

Further testing recommended under variable stress conditions.

Her eyes skimmed the headers that followed.

PHASE II TRIALS.

EMOTIONAL ENTRAINMENT.

COGNITIVE BLEED.

The words seemed to hum on the page. They vibrated faintly under the kitchen light. She ran a finger along the edge of one chart, brainwave patterns, oscillating in perfect rhythm. The caption read:

Induced alignment through

environmental resonance.

Her stomach twisted. *Environmental resonance.* The hum in the walls. The vibration under her feet. The kitchen light flickered, a faint tremor moving through the floor. The house exhaled... or maybe it only felt that way.

She flipped to the final page. It bore a single paragraph, typed cleanly, methodically:

Project EIDOLON establishes

proof of concept for cross-

perceptual communication through

emotional frequency modulation.

Field subjects demonstrate

profound psychological pliability

within contained environments.

Sustained exposure yields

irreversible cognitive integration.

Her reflection wavered in the polished surface of the table, pale and still. The hum beneath the floorboards deepened, threading through the walls like a pulse. She pressed her palm flat against the last page. The paper felt warm.

And in that warmth, something answered her touch, something faint, but alive.

One note read:

"Subject began perceiving

movement in peripheral vision

within 12 hours of exposure to

encoded environmental stimuli.

Hallucinations intensified alongside

emotional agitation.

Recommended duration: 72-hour

continuous saturation."

Another:

"Fear is the threshold. The brain's survival response must be exceeded for doors to open. Perception widens under distress."

She turned the page. There, in type, was Aubrey's name.

Dr. Aubrey Bainbridge —Lead, Phase II Behavioral Integration Study.
PROJECT EIDOLON: NEURAL RETUNING — SUBJECT: G. BAINBRIDGE

G. BAINBRIDGE. Was that *her*? Was *she* the lab rat? The name looked wrong on the page, alien, as though it belonged to someone else entirely. Yet the longer she stared, the more the letters seemed to settle into her skin. Her vision blurred.

The paper crackled under her trembling hands. Each sheet smelled faintly of toner, antiseptic, and something older, something she couldn't name, a scent that lived somewhere between chemical sterilization and decay.

She lifted the page closer to the light. The diagram detailed cross-sections of the human brain, each part labeled in clinical shorthand:

Limbic Stimulation, Auditory Entrainment, Memory Suppression.

Her breath quickened. Tiny annotations lined the margins, written in Aubrey's unmistakable handwriting. The ink strokes cut into the paper, forceful and certain.

Subject displays measurable compliance increase within 48 hours. Auditory hallucinations no longer distressing, subject demonstrates adaptive response. Emotional dependency successfully established.

Her stomach clenched. She turned the page. Another image, EEG patterns, waveforms rising and falling in synchronized rhythm. The caption beneath read:

Emotional frequency alignment achieved through environmental saturation.

Environmental saturation. Her throat went dry. The next page contained an authorization signature. **Aubrey Bainbridge, MD, PhD.** The stamp beneath bore the emblem of Bainbridge Research Institute. The faded ink carried the color of rust. Her pulse thundered in her ears.

She could almost hear his voice behind the clinical phrasing, smooth and detached. *You're overwrought again, Gabriella. I do worry about you.*

The papers slipped from her fingers. They scattered across the table like fallen leaves. Some slid to the floor, edges curling where moisture from her palms had soaked through.

She stared down at the diagram, the clean, precise lines mapping out her mind as though it were a machine he had built. In ways, it was. Not theory. Not research.

Her. The subject was her.

"NEURAL INDUCTION ZONE — P2 ACCESS POINT"

And next to it, underlined twice:

"Unknown Contact Structure."

Below that, a handwritten margin note in faint pencil:

What Hayes called the Thin Place. Reyland's work was closer than we thought.

Her vision blurred. *Reyland Hayes.* The man who built this house. Who used fear to fracture minds and glimpse other realities, and Aubrey's work mirrored his almost exactly.

Another page below it had what appeared to be blueprints to her house. There were strange indicators throughout, but she couldn't see anything unusual when she examined the areas.

It wasn't coincidence. It was *inheritance.* She dropped the papers. The whispers in the house surged. It became a roar so deep the walls vibrated.

The hallway mirror darkened. The wallpaper curled slightly at the edges, as if it recoiled from something she couldn't see. She heard deep groans in the home that sounded like an ancient tree moving in the wind.

She stood there, frozen, as a shape passed through the reflection in the nearby mirror. Thin. Male. Watching. The lights flickered once. Then again. Somewhere beneath her, deep in the bones of the house, something breathed.

She turned slowly. The diary lay open on the kitchen table, its pages fluttering though there was no breeze. It knew what she'd read. And it was waiting to be understood.

Chapter 29

Her fingers trembled as she traced the slanted script across the brittle diary pages. The air was thick, not just with dust, but with attention. The house seemed to watch, silent and patient. She sat cross-legged on the study floor, by the window.

Allura's words bled across the page, each one soaked in grief and dread. Through them, a life emerged, one consumed by fear, betrayal, and the slow decay of sanity.

Dr. Reyland Hayes, the house's original master, had begun as a healer, a respected physician. But line by line, his image warped into something monstrous. His notes were clinical, detached, each sentence a window into a mind convinced of its own righteousness.

> *Fear is the key. To break the mind is to understand its deepest truths. They will thank me when I'm finished, even if they do not understand now. Even if they scream.*

The words were written with eerie precision, as though he documented a cure rather than cruelty. Her stomach twisted. Hayden had experimented not with chemicals, but with emotion. He stripped his subjects to their bare terror. He amplified. He observed how long before they broke. His "subjects" weren't volunteers. Friends. Patients. Those who trusted him most.

Her pulse quickened as realization seeped in. She cried harder. The parallels to Aubrey were unmistakable. The same fascination with human thresholds. The same evasions. The same absence. A cold breeze stirred the oddly stale air.

"Charlie?" she whispered.

No answer.

She waited. She stood there for a long time. The ceiling seemed to spin overhead. Francis's voice echoed in her mind. *He's playing with fire. Get out before it's too late.*

She missed Francis. She had the worst feeling about her death. Like it was deliberate. Could Aubrey have caused that, too? Or was that idea spawned by her unraveling? She stared at the papers, but her brain was far away. *Heart failure?* Or something worse. The attic door creaked overhead.

James waited at his door when she arrived that evening. Concern etched into his face. His house was warm, the opposite of hers, full of life and gentle clutter. She told him everything, the diary, the letters, the parallels to Aubrey's research. He listened, his frown deepening as she spoke.

When she finished, he flipped through the papers, his expression grim. "He wasn't studying fear," he said finally. "He was summoning it. Or feeding it."

She shivered. "And Aubrey's continuing it. Whether he knows it or not."

He leaned forward, voice low and sure. "Then we find proof. Whatever he's hiding, it will probably be mirrored in that house."

They began the next morning. Daylight softened the house's edges, but the air inside was still thick, charged, as if daylight had only muted its awareness, not banished it.

They searched In the attic. Dust coated their hands, the scent of mildew heavy in the air. She heard fingers hit something metal. "Here," he said. He pulled out a tarnished box. Inside lay rusted keys, yellowed papers, and a sealed envelope stamped with wax.

The letters inside were fragile, the ink fading, but the words still legible.

You've invited them in, and they've taken root. I fear they will never let us leave.

Her throat tightened. "She knew." She saw something glint down below the dirt on the floor. She reached down and pulled up a piece of jewelry. It was an old locket.

James's gaze met hers. "And Aubrey... he's following Hayden."

The attic temperature plunged. Their breath misted in the air. Then, a whisper. "Gabby." She turned sharply. Charlie stood in the corner, eyes wide, pale light pooling around him. "He's coming," he said softly. "And he doesn't want you here."

The attic door slammed shut. Darkness swallowed them.

James caught her arm. "We're leaving," he hissed.

The shadows surged, writhing like smoke alive. Whispers rose, overlapping into a single voice, one vast, angry exhalation. She froze. Her eyes fixed on Charlie. His outline flickered, his expression full of sorrow.

"I'm sorry," he whispered. "I tried to warn you."

Then he was gone. The shadows lunged. James pulled her toward the stairs. The two of them stumbled down the old stairs, half-blind. The darkness pressed close until they reached the daylight at the front door.

She fell to her knees, gasping. The diary was still in her hands, its pages fluttering in the wind like trapped birds. The locket was around her wrist. The house loomed behind them, silent and watching.

She knew now that it wasn't haunted. It was inhabited. Whatever Hayden had invited inside a century ago had never left. And if Aubrey had awakened it again, then it wanted more than their fear.

James admitted to seeing it all, before he left. It wasn't just her. It wasn't unraveling. He was there and saw Charlie and the horrible shadow. She nearly collapsed with relief after he was gone. Someone else had experienced it. She might be a little unraveled, but nowhere near the level she feared.

That night, she couldn't sleep. She scrubbed the locket and chain until it looked new. Apparently, it was real. She was grateful to whomever locked the attic. So much of the Hayes' history could've been gone forever if tenants had frequented it.

She roamed the house in quiet loops, notebook in hand, recording everything she remembered. When she reached the basement door. She paused at the top of the stairs.

The noise was back. Not from the walls this time, from something mechanical. She crept down, the flashlight beam shaking slightly. There, along the back wall, half-shrouded in shadow, sat the water softener Aubrey had installed months ago.

She crouched, running her fingers along the metal base. She guessed it was the water softener, but it looked strange. It was installed at the water heater. There. A logo. Small, etched into the corner. The same as Aubrey's lab. She stumbled back. The hum deepened in response. The Bainbridge Institute did not make appliances. So, what was this?

Another package arrived the next morning. No postage. No return address. Just a manila envelope, thick with paper. Inside:

PROJECT EIDOLON– PHASE I

Neurological Entrainment Trials –

INTERNAL DOCUMENTS

Her hands shook as she flipped through. Diagrams of brainwave patterns. Reports on emotional saturation. Redacted subjects. She knew she'd had an EEG at the hospital, at Aubrey's urging, the year before. It was just a screen for potential epileptic anomalies, or so he said. Some of the scans, however, were far more recent. A month earlier. Two months earlier. How did he get them when she never had them done?

And then, Aubrey's name.

Dr. Aubrey Bainbridge — Phase II Lead

Handwritten notes followed:

Hayes reached the wall. We will break through it.

The basement. The device. The whispers in the attic. It wasn't coincidence. It was the plan.

Chapter 30

The house felt heavier the next day. It pressed against her chest as though it breathed in time with her. It didn't creak with age anymore; it sighed with purpose.

Every sound, the whisper of the wind, the stretch of the old beams, felt sharpened. Intentional. The house wasn't merely haunted. It was attentive. Participating.

She scrolled through her phone, opened a book, stared at the wallpaper's curling edges. Anything to distract herself. She kept returning to the anonymous documents. *Project EIDOLON.* The water softener with Aubrey's lab logo. And the locket she'd found in the attic... Alura's.

And Aubrey... He hadn't met James. He didn't know the neighbors. And yet, he'd mentioned James by name several times. *"I see you're spending quite a bit of time with your new friend, James."*

She hadn't responded. She didn't know what to say. Obviously, someone was watching her to know that. It gave her chills to think that some was spying on her. Did he know someone in a nearby house? Were the neighbors watching her? Or was it James himself? That was also possible.

Her silence had been met with static. It made her head hurt. She needed to do something. She stood. She grabbed the flashlight from her nightstand. Her movements felt sluggish, like wading through water. The hallway pressed inward. She needed to explore the attic further. She knew it was safe. And it was filled with who knew what.

The attic door was ajar. She didn't remember leaving it that way. She pushed it farther open. The hinges groaned, low and agonized. The flashlight flicked across boxes and draped mirrors. The house went quiet again. Her breath misted in the icy air. A forgotten season lived up here. Then, something caught the light.

A strange metal panel bolted into the wall near the rafters, far down in the corner. It was newer than anything else in the attic. She crept closer. It bore the same logo from the lab. Aubrey's lab.

Her stomach dropped. Something behind the wall shifted. She staggered back. The flashlight died. Utter black. And then: a whisper, no breath to carry it: "Gabriella."

The air thickened. A presence stood behind her. The flashlight flickered with its words. She turned, expecting Charlie. Instead, Father had shape.

Ryland was tall. Elongated. She thought of the Slenderman depictions. His features blurred, like wet ink on paper. But his presence, terrible and full, was unmistakable. Father. The same thing that grabbed her ankle.

His arm reached towards her. The air cracked with pressure. She turned to run but something caught her. He took her breath as she felt her body lift off the floor. Her body flew backwards, like a marionette, slammed into the attic wall. Pain shot through her spine. Her scream caught in her throat. The house groaned.

She looked through the closest grimy attic window. She couldn't move. Outside, James parked his car and approached his front door. She tried to will him to rescue her.

Father unleashed another roar and make the house vibrate. There was a thump. Then the crash. She was thankful that he obviously heard something. He dropped his bag of groceries and sprinted to her house.

She screamed and could only hope he heard. She still couldn't move. She could barely breathe. Was she paralyzed? Or was it the demon... or whatever it was. She heard James shout her name, but she didn't know if he could hear her respond. She still had the doors locked.

She heard a pause and then the front door was kicked open. She heard wood splinter. Before she could yell, she was lifted again. She was flung across to the other side of the attic. Her head hit hard. Her vision tunneled.

Then James's voice: "Gabriella!"

It seemed like seconds later she was in his arms. The shadows shrieked at his presence. They recoiled from the light that spilled up the stairs. He carried her down the stairs. Her limp form pressed against his chest. He didn't stop until they were outside. Until the cold air and silence wrapped around them like a shroud. The world went black.

She woke in James's guest bed. The morning was light thin and gray through the curtains. He brought her tea; his expression carved with worry.

"I didn't know what else to do," he said.

She sat up slowly, head pounding. "Thank you."

He hesitated. "You shouldn't go back there."

She sipped the tea. The warmth steadied her. "I have to. It's my home."

James looked stricken. "That house nearly killed you."

"I know," she said. "But I can't unravel. If I leave, I don't know what Aubrey will do." She couldn't prove he was responsible for Francis's death, but she grew more and more convinced each day that he was. Leaving may stop what was in motion, but it was more likely to become worse. She didn't want an innocent person being caught up in it.

She returned that afternoon. Alone. James already had workmen installing a new door. The hall beyond it silent. Too silent. No groaning beams. No whispering pipes. No scratching. The house was absolutely still. Like it was waiting. It would be quiet for the time being. Whatever was there didn't want an audience.

She stepped farther in. Slow. Quiet. She breathed deep. The air smelled like dust and something older. She pressed a palm to the wall. It still felt warm, but she didn't know why. She asked one of the women to see if he thought it was unusual.

Both of them checked most of the walls. They told her to remain vigilant. Old houses could hide fire under the plaster.

That's not the only thing hidden under the plaster, she thought. She started to make a joke about the bones in the attic but didn't. That might be too much.

She breathed deep. The air smelled like dust and something older. She wandered from room to room, softly calling Charlie's name. But it wasn't Charlie who answered. In mirrors, she caught a glimpse, not of a boy or a man, but a woman. Always in motion. Always fading. A hand brushing a doorknob. A face just beyond her reflection.

Allura.

She stood in front of the master bedroom mirror, staring. For a breathless moment, she swore she saw another figure beside her. Then, only her own face stared back. And yet, the scent of lavender hung faintly in the air. Not hers. Alura's. The house wasn't angry now. It was remembering. And something was reaching through that remembrance to find her.

Chapter 31

She took James a copy of her key in case he needed it. Maybe she should stay with James. She was often uneasy in the house, but she was downright afraid that evening. She couldn't shake the sense that eyes watched her. From above. From the hall. From the seams where two walls met like pressed lips. The sensation crawled across her skin in slow, deliberate strokes.

She checked the attic earlier, while the workmen repaired the door. She *knew* what she'd seen when James carried her out: broken lathing, bowed studs, the wall gouged as though something inside had tried to tear its way free. A physical record of the thing that had cornered her.

But now? Nothing. No trace of the violence that had happened there. It was as if the house had healed.

She ran her hands lightly along her arms. The bruises there bloomed in mottled violets and yellows, fingerprints of pressure she couldn't fully explain. The house had reset itself, erased its injuries, yet she still bore hers.

"Too bad I'm not as repairable," she muttered under her breath. She retreated to the living room. She didn't even want to be in her bedroom. The couch felt safer, if safety was even still a concept she believed in. At least here she had doors within sight, windows she could throw open if something moved too fast in the dark.

The air felt colder than the thermostat read. The vents whispered in inconsistent drafts, like the house inhaled and exhaled on an unpredictable rhythm. Even the wallpaper seemed alive tonight, its curling edges flexing like the peeling skin of something once-human.

She tried to distract herself: scrolled through her phone, opened a book, checked her email inbox three times. But her focus blurred, her gaze drifting back, again and again, to the anonymous packet of documents spread across the coffee table.

Project EIDOLON.

The name alone made her stomach twist. She lifted the papers again, fingertips tracing the edges. Cold to the touch, as if they carried the chill of wherever they'd been before landing on her doorstep.

She was becoming much better at reading the lab documents. One page detailed a substance capable of inducing dissociation and receptive states, phrased clinically enough to hide how horrifying it really was. Another diagram mapped a theoretical distribution system integrated into municipal water lines. Did the Bainbridge Institute really plan on sending whatever that substance was into the public water system?

Her eyes flicked toward the basement, toward the water softener. She had to tilt the flashlight just right to see it, faint as a watermark. Aubrey's lab didn't even *make* appliances. It was a chemical lab. The sting of betrayal felt fresh again, sharp enough to make her chest ache.

Her gaze landed on the locket she'd placed beside the documents. Alura's locket. The metal had warmed to the temperature of her palm earlier in the evening, though she'd barely touched it. Now it sat innocently under the glow of the lamp, its chain coiled like a sleeping snake.

She swallowed. There were too many connections. Too many overlapping secrets. Everything kept pointing back to the house, to Aubrey, to something older than both. To possibilities just as old.

James had stayed with her until dusk. He'd been kind, gentle even, doing small things she hadn't realized she needed. Double-checking locks, turning on lights, even setting a glass of water on the table. But something in her had begun to recoil at closeness, even the safe kind. The edge Aubrey had carved into her made it hard to accept anything soft without bracing for pain.

They'd stood near the window, golden light slipping across James's features. His concern had been so clear, so earnest, that it made her chest tighten.

"James," she had said quietly, careful not to break the fragile moment. "I'm grateful for everything. Really. But I hope it's okay that... I just need a friend right now."

He blinked. The slight disappointment was visible, a ripple through his gentle expression. After a pause, he nodded. "Of course," he said. "I just want you safe."

She'd forced a small smile, the best she could manage. "Me too."

Now, hours later, she replayed the conversation. Her fingers tapped anxiously against her knee. The house groaned in response, as though echoing her tension.

A faint sound drifted from upstairs, a whispering scrape, like fingernails trailing down a wall. Her whole body stiffened. She held her breath, waiting. Listening. Another sound. A soft *tap*. Then silence. The bruises on her arms ached, as though remembering those unseen hands.

Outside, the wind pushed against the windows. The house answered with a slow creak that sounded terribly close to a sigh. She laid down on the sofa and turned the television on. "If it wants to finish the job," she whispered, "it can try."

The house settled around her. The lights flickered once, twice, as though deciding something. And somewhere upstairs, light as breath, something moved.

Chapter 32

She woke with the locket clenched in her palm. The scattered documents whispered faintly as the air shifted. Somewhere deep in the house, a door creaked open, soft, deliberate, and her pulse stuttered.

She didn't want to move. Didn't want to disturb the fragile barrier between what was real and what wasn't. Because lately, she wasn't sure. She had begun seeing things. Shapes behind doors. Flickers of white along the stairs. Not Charlie. Not anymore. These were different. Older.

She went to brush her teeth and change. She stumbled into a chair by the entrance to the foyer. The scrape of the chair against the floor was deafening in the silence. The air was heavy, humid, almost alive. The locket's cold weight anchored her as she crossed the hall.

Her feet faltered at the first step of the staircase. The oppressive stillness vibrated with expectation. Halfway up, a draft slid over her skin, cold, unnatural. Her eyes lifted. The attic door stood ajar. Just enough for the dark to breathe.

She darted into the master bedroom to freshen up and change. It was still partially open when she came out of the bedroom. Something moved inside, a flicker, a suggestion of form, gone when she blinked. Her breath caught.

She took another step closer. Her fingers brushed the wall for balance. "Charlie?" she whispered. Silence. The quiet pressed back, thick and solid. And then...*Knock. Knock. Knock.*

The sound came from downstairs, sharp and insistent. She nearly stumbled; her heart dropped to her stomach. She ran. The doorknob was cold beneath her hand as she hesitated, then pulled.

173

James stood on the porch. The porch light cast his face in soft gold. Concern carved deep lines into his expression. "Gabriella," he said quickly. "I just wanted to make sure you're alright."

She blinked. Relief and embarrassment warred in her chest. "I'm fine," she said automatically, stepping aside. "Or trying to be."

He entered cautiously, his eyes sweeping the dim space. "Something feels... different," he murmured. "Heavier."

Her voice cracked. "You feel it too?"

He met her gaze. "Yeah. Whatever this house is, it's awake."

Her throat tightened. "It's not just the house, James. It's Aubrey. It's all connected. I can't explain it, but...."

"You don't have to," he said, steady and calm. "You don't have to face this alone. We'll get you out. Start fresh."

She shook her head. "You don't understand. It won't let me go. Not until all this is resolved."

Before he could respond, something *shifted*. Her eyes unfocused. The hallway stretched, blurred at the edges. The wallpaper melted into tiled walls, the air smelling suddenly of iodine and bleach.

Then she saw it. Not the present. The past. And down a familiar hallway, a voice. Francis. She wasn't walking but floating, like a dream, through the old hospital space. She saw Francis and Aubrey, clearly, at Bainbridge estate.

"You said it was only theory," Francis hissed.

"Theory becomes practice," Aubrey replied coolly.

"She has been a wonderful wife for you."

"She has been a perfect blank slate." He spoke as if she were a burden.

"How could you treat her that way? Why? She never did anything to you... except love you."

"She has never known me to love me. Not in years."

"Who's fault is that?"

"This will ensure our product is flawless."

"Only if you get away with it."

"We aren't doing anything to 'get away with'."

"You know exactly what you're doing."

"Father would've approved."

"Listen to yourself. *Father?* We were commodities, not family. Since when did his work matter any to you? You should know that. Why do you think you're siblings fled as soon as they could?"

"They were weak. I intend to become even greater than father ever was."

"I think you need to check the definition of great. The only people who remember your father's great and all-important work are those who got a nice check when he died. Science and medicine forgot him entirely." Francis slapped a stack of papers against his chest. "You're hurting her. You're using her. I won't allow it. Grant her the divorce and get away from her."

His eyes turned cold. "You have no idea what I'm trying to do."

She turned to leave. He shoved her. Francis hit a metal table with a sickening crack and collapsed. Her body didn't move. The vision shattered.

She gasped. She collapsed to her knees. James caught her.

"Gabriella!"

She looked up at him, her eyes wide, tears blurring the edges. "I saw her."

"Who?"

"Francis. He killed her." James froze. Above them, slow footsteps began again. They turned their heads upward. The attic.

This time, they climbed without speaking. The door stood wide open. The attic was dim. Moonlight poured through the small window, turning the dust in the air to drifting silver.

And then she saw it. *Him.* A figure. Standing in the corner. Human-shaped. But wrong. Its outline seemed to breathe, stretching too far, shrinking again, like it couldn't hold itself together.

James's voice was a whisper. "Do you see that?"

She nodded. She couldn't look away. The figure shifted. The darkness around it rippled. Then it spoke.

"You shouldn't have come." The sound was layered, a whisper and a growl and a sigh, all at once.

He pulled her close as the figure unraveled. Its shape collapsed into a thousand black tendrils that whipped through the air like smoke caught in a storm. They curled, twisted, then vanished into the floor.

Silence.

The attic was empty again. James turned, his face pale. "We're leaving," he said.

This time, she didn't argue. They fled down the stairs, through the front hall, out into the cold night. The air outside was thin, biting, clean.

She stopped at the edge of the porch, her chest heaving. The house loomed behind them, still and vast, its windows glinting faintly in the moonlight.

It didn't need to move to feel alive. She clutched the locket in her fist. Her pulse pounded beneath the metal. She knew. It wasn't done with her. It was waiting. And it would not let her go until she understood what it wanted.

Chapter 33

Another package waited on her doorstep. Small. Plain. Unmarked. She hesitated before touching it, and a cold weight gathered in her gut. Something about it felt wrong. It was too heavy in a way that wasn't physical. She lifted it anyway, her hands trembled as she carried it inside.

At the kitchen table, she unwrapped the paper with slow, deliberate fingers. Inside was another stack of documents, bound with a black ribbon. The paper smelled faintly metallic, like old coins and antiseptic.

Across the top, in bold block letters:

PROJECT EIDOLON

Her pulse picked up. The language was clinical, emotionless, but the implications were monstrous. A chemical agent, distributed through air or water, designed to manipulate neural responses, induce fear, obedience, and compliance. Not a weapon in the traditional sense, but an emotional contagion.

In small doses: paranoia,

hallucinations, panic.

In larger ones: paralysis. Silence.

Oblivion. Death.

It was written as though human suffering were a process, not a crime. Her trembling fingers turned each page. Field tests. Dosage tables. Experiment logs. She didn't notice the tear rolling down her cheek until it hit the paper, bleeding the ink.

Then…

Project Contributors and Consultants.

Her eyes stopped. Her heart didn't.

Dr. Aubrey Bainbridge

She blinked once. Twice. But it didn't change. His name was there, printed clearly beneath the government insignia. The room tilted. The world, her world, tilted. The final page was handwritten. His handwriting. If successful, Project EIDOLON will secure unprecedented funding and influence.

The words looked alien. Detached. The penmanship she once found graceful now felt surgical, like incisions made without anesthesia. She whispered his name, barely audible. "Aubrey…"

The sound vanished into the air, swallowed by the house. Then…a voice behind her. "You shouldn't read things you don't understand."

She froze. Turned.

Aubrey stood in the doorway. His face was calm. Too calm. He wore his usual dark coat, unbuttoned, his hair damp as though he'd just come from the rain.

"How... how long have you been home?" she stammered.

He smiled faintly. "Long enough."

His tone was soft. Gentle. But the stillness in his eyes was something else, something fixed, analytical. She slid the top page over the rest. "Did you send this?"

"Send what?" he asked.

"This package?"

He glanced at the documents. "No. But I suppose you've seen what you wanted to see."

"You're the lead for the project?"

He laughed softly. It was strange, merely performative. "I'm listed on hundreds of things, Gabriella. Half the time, I don't even know which ones."

Her voice trembled. "This one was about fear."

He tilted his head. "Everything is about fear."

Something in the room shifted. The shadows thickened, edging closer to his feet like loyal dogs. He didn't notice or pretended not to. "I want you to rest," he said quietly. "You're exhausted. I can hear it in your voice."

"You killed Francis," she blurted. "I saw it. I saw you."

He blinked once, slowly. "Did you?"

She opened her mouth to answer, but her voice faltered. The memory was already smearing around the edges, like ink bleeding into water. She remembered the crash, the blood, but maybe it was the house, not reality.

Aubrey stepped closer. His hand brushed her shoulder. "You've been through a lot. I'm not your enemy."

Her chest tightened. "You sound like you rehearsed it."

His expression didn't change. "If I were rehearsing, you'd already know how it ends." Then he turned and left the kitchen, his footsteps deliberate and slow.

When the door closed behind him, she realized she hadn't heard his car leave. She felt faint again. The light over the table flickered once, then steadied. The papers before her blurred, the typeface rippling like it was breathing. She blinked hard, trying to focus…and the kitchen was gone.

She stood in the old hospital upstairs. Not as it was now, but as it was then. The walls were tile and plaster, lined with beds. The air reeked of disinfectants and rot. Distant screams echoed through the corridors.

A woman passed, her gown torn, her hair loose around her shoulders. Alura. Gabriella reached out, but her hand passed through her.

The ghost moved like smoke. It paced beside an empty bed. She was a ghost of herself. Her hair was unkempt. Her gown was tattered and stained. Her lips moved soundlessly, until she turned. Now her eyes locked with Gabriella's. And suddenly she could hear her. "He promised to cure the mind. But he only wanted to break it."

The walls trembled. Lights flared. For an instant, Gabriella saw herself reflected in the glass door opposite, except it wasn't her. The reflection smiled, calm and knowing, before flickering out.

She shoved the papers behind the cabinet drawer beside her. She didn't want Aubrey to get them. She didn't know what was happening to her, but she was in no shape to stay ahead of him and protect paperwork. There was no way in hell she would risk the study's desk with him still here.

She gasped and stumbled back, clutching the locket. Alura was gone. The hospital walls bled back into wallpaper. The lights dimmed. Was that to be where this all went?

Her pulse thundered. She could taste metal. The house seemed to vibrate, humming low, steady, as if it approved.

She whispered into the dark. "What do you want from me?" The house answered with a slow creak.

In the reflection of the darkened window, she saw a shape behind her. Long hair, pale skin, hands clasped like she was praying. Alura again, faint and flickering. But when she turned, she was alone.

Outside, wind rattled the shutters. The temperature dropped sharply, the air tasting of rain and static. She sank to the floor. The quiet was suffocating. She clumsily stuffed the locket into the silverware drawer. She didn't want Aubrey to have that, either.

Then a whisper rose through the walls, not cruel, but weary. "You are almost where I was."

She didn't know if the visions were gifts or warnings. But she knew this: the house was showing her its truth.

Chapter 34

She forced herself upright, every movement a war against the invisible weight pressing her into the mattress. Her body ached like she'd been thrown from a height, because she had.

Evidently, insomnia wasn't a problem any longer. She still felt so sleepy. The air was cold and thick, dense like submerged water, pressing into her lungs with each breath. And Aubrey stood beside the bed. A glass of water in one hand. A small white pill in the other.

The residual sleepiness vanished. The shadows behind him weren't still. They coiled and stretched, not in response to light, but intention.

"I don't need that," she rasped. Her voice cracked in her dry throat. "I'll be fine."

His face didn't soften. Instead, a flicker of irritation broke through the smooth, measured mask he always wore. He set the glass down hard enough that the rim rang against the wood.

"Stop being stubborn, Gabriella," he said, voice low, cold, rehearsed. "You look like hell. I'm only trying to help you. So take the pill."

It wasn't care. It was control. She looked at the water. It shimmered, but not from movement. The surface shifted faintly, like there was something inside it. Something alive.

Don't. The word pulsed in her mind, soft and clear. Her eyes met his. There was no kindness left. Just the sharp, unreadable gleam of someone watching a test subject fail to comply.

"I don't trust you," she said, barely above a whisper.

Aubrey smiled, cruel and dismissive. "*Trust* me?" His tone sharpened. "That's rich. You've been whispering behind my back. James. Francis. Everyone. You made me look like the villain." He took a slow step closer. The shadows moved with him.

"If I'm the villain," she said, her voice trembling but firm, "then it's because you made me one."

He paused. Tilted his head. The smile faded into something empty. "You're right," he said. "I'm not the man you married." He leaned in slightly. "And I never was."

The air behind him buckled. The shadows bent inward, twitching like a muscle beneath skin. Then... a whisper at her ear. Soft. Innocent. Familiar. *"Don't take it."*

Charlie. Her heart surged. She grabbed the pill, put it in her mouth, and used her tongue to push it up between her teeth and cheek. She took a sip of water and pretended to swallow it. He seemed pleased, "There. Now, get some rest."

She laid back down and he left the room. She spat the pill out and threw it in the trash can by the bed. Now it was a waiting game.

She sat up and went to the bathroom. She listened to see if she could hear where he was. All of her documents pertaining to his work and his habits was locked away in the desk. She hoped he didn't break into it.

Oddly enough, it sounded like he paced overhead. Back and forth, with no real destination. She scrolled on her phone and played some games. He didn't return to check on her. Thankfully. Around an hour later, she heard his car come to life and drive away.

She should've installed those security cameras. She could've kicked herself for forgetting. Now, it could be too late. Who knew how long he'd been in the house while she slept? He might not be back for any length of time for weeks, or more.

He would eventually be back. She knew. The house wasn't finished with either of them.

Chapter 35

It wasn't just the house anymore. It was Aubrey. Whatever bound him to this place had deepened, rooted, fused. He didn't live in the house, he *inhabited* it. Or perhaps, it inhabited him. Maybe they had a symbiotic relationship.

Her limbs felt like lead. Her skin burned cold. The exhaustion wasn't fatigue anymore. It was depletion. Like the house was feeding, not on blood or body, but on will. The flu that had come and went threw an more powerful punch now. Was this the unraveling? Would Eidophrene kill her?

She needed to leave but didn't think she could. She didn't feel like she could make it to the front door. She held Allura's diary and her locket laid on the pillow next to her. She didn't remember retrieving either. She couldn't remember coming back to bed or even what day it was.

Then, a sound. The bedroom doorknob rattled. Sharp. Mechanical. Deliberate. She froze, heart stuttering in her chest. The rattling stopped. Then... three slow knocks.

"Gabriella." Aubrey's voice. Low. Soft. Authoritative. "Open the door."

"I can't," she whispered.

She just heard him leave, didn't she? She hadn't heard him return. She didn't move. The space between them buzzed, electrified. She could feel him out there, not just standing, but *pressing*. Like his presence alone bent the air.

"I know you're in there." His voice almost crooned. "We need to talk."

She clutched the diary tighter. Her mind swirled with the visions, the project documents, the locket, the tunnel. All of it pointed to one conclusion:

Aubrey wasn't Aubrey. And he didn't come to talk. The doorknob turned. Why had he jiggled it like it was locked? The door opened.

Aubrey stepped inside, half in shadow, half in soft lamplight. His smile looked rehearsed, not kind. His eyes scanned the room, then landed on her. "Why are you hiding from me?"

"I wasn't," she said, standing slowly. "I'm sleepy."

He stepped forward. The shadows bent with him. "You've been thinking."

He glanced at the diary in her hands. "My word, that old book? You shouldn't go prying. It's dangerous, Gabriella. There are things in this house, in you, better left undisturbed."

Her breath came shallow. "You mean things like Project EIDOLON?"

His smile faltered. A flicker of something passed behind his eyes, rage, maybe. Or fear. "You've been poisoned by your own paranoia."

"I'm *awake.*"

They stood in silence. And then he said, gently: "You're part of it now. It doesn't matter what you believe."

Something behind him shifted, a ripple in the shadows. She needed to move. Something was different. Now, he scared her more than Father. If she submitted to her weariness, she would die. She knew it.

She made herself stand, in spite of her pain. In spite of Aubrey's protests. She wasn't particularly shocked to see Charlie at the end of the hallway. His eyes locked on hers. His lips moved in silence:

Run.

She didn't wait. She bolted, pushing past Aubrey. His hand grazed her shoulder, ice-cold, but she tore away and sprinted down the hallway.

Doors slammed around her. The floor buckled beneath her feet. The house twisted, *reacting.* She didn't head for the front door. She ran towards the attic. The idea came not from reason, but instinct, something Charlie had once said. Something about where Allura had hidden her last entries. Where he had kept her. Where it began.

She reached the top of the stairs. She nearly tripped as she threw the door open. The attic air was thick, humid. Breathing felt like drowning.

But something was different now. The far wall, where the strange metal panel had been, was gone. In its place, a hallway. It hadn't been there before. A narrow corridor of white and gray walls, half-crumbling, half-sanitized. A forgotten wing. A hospital wing.

Fluorescent lights flickered overhead, buzzing like flies. She stepped inside, each step echoed too loudly. She passed empty beds, rusted IV stands, machines that hadn't functioned in decades. But the walls were clean, too clean.

She turned a corner, and the world *shifted*. Suddenly, she was in the past, not just observing. Voices echoed down the hall. She crept toward them, her body cold, her breath fogging the air. Charlie appeared beside her. Tears filled her eyes. "Is it real?"

He nodded. "All of it. He kept this wing hidden. Said it was condemned. But this is where it started. Father. Mother. Aubrey. All of them."

"Why are you showing me this?"

"Because it's your turn," he whispered. And then he was gone.

She knelt alone in the hallway of ghosts. The air pulsed. The hum returned, louder now. She stood, heart pounding. She wasn't running this time. She was going to finish it. Whatever "it" was. Death was better than panic.

She braced herself for confrontation, but she blinked. Suddenly the attic was normal. Charlie was gone. The attic just felt empty. Of everything.

She returned downstairs to confront Aubrey. If he wanted a fight, he was getting one. She checked all the rooms on the second floor.

She went down to the first level. The rooms were empty. He wasn't there. She ran to the front door. Aubrey's car wasn't in the drive. She returned to her bedroom. The diary and locket were gone. There was no water glass on her nightstand. She ran to the study and unlocked the desk. Everything was where she put it.

My God, a chill ran down her spine. What was going on? Was it Eidophrene... or her?

Chapter 36

Her dreams had always been uneasy, but now they were *alive*. Every night, the house found her, reaching across distance and darkness to drag her back into its arms. It smelled like mildew and old blood. She felt the cold fingers of the shadows as they crept around her limbs, whispering in tongues she didn't know but somehow understood.

The shadows in her dreams coiled like smoke. They whispered her name through the walls. And Aubrey was always there. His smile. His eyes. That voice, like silk stretched too thin.

"You can't leave me," he murmured. "We belong to the house."

She'd wake gasping, drenched in sweat so cold it felt like she'd been underwater. Her chest would ache with panic, her sheets tangled tight like bindings.

At first, she told herself they were nightmares, residue from trauma. But then she began to wake in strange places. The first time, she was barefoot in the open doorway at 3:33 A.M. The doorknob was icy in her palm. Her feet streaked with dirt and grass. Her hands bore faint scratches, as though she'd been digging. She didn't remember leaving bed.

Then came the whispers. Soft at first. A roar beneath the walls. Then words, fragmented and distant. *Come back... Come home...* They followed her everywhere, echoing in the soft whine of the refrigerator, the creak of old pipes, the breath between heartbeats.

It got so bad she asked James if she could stay in his guest room again. When she told James about everything, her voice trembled. "It's like the house is alive," she said. "Like it's reaching for me, even here."

He didn't argue. His expression darkened. "Maybe it's not just the house," he said quietly. "Maybe Aubrey... left something behind." The thought chilled her more than anything. But deep down, she knew he was right. Leaving wouldn't free her. It had only stretched the tether.

That night, Charlie returned to her in the strange room. She couldn't decipher if it were real, or if she were dreaming. He stood in the corner of her bedroom, pale and flickering, the light barely clinging to his form. His small hands were clenched at his sides. "Miss Gabriella," he whispered. "You have to go back."

Her pulse fluttered. "Back? Charlie, I can't. It's—"

"You don't understand," he said. "It won't let you go. The experiment isn't finished. The house is alive. It's feeding off him... and off you."

Her voice caught. "Feeding?"

"It grows stronger when you're afraid," Charlie said. "When you stay away, it gets angry. That's why it's reaching for you."

Her stomach turned. "What happens if I don't go back?"

Charlie's gaze dropped. "Then you won't survive. Father never leaves an experiment undone."

Chapter 37

By dawn, her resolve had solidified like bone. Fear sat in her stomach like a stone, but beneath it, something older burned, something fierce. When she turned into the long, cracked driveway, the structure rose before her like a mausoleum. Its black windows gleamed in the overcast light, vacant and watchful.

Inside, the air clung to her skin, damp, metallic, sharp. The house exhaled around her with each footstep. The wood beneath her shoes groaned, not with age, but with anticipation.

She stopped at the desk and then straight to the basement. The diary was clutched tight in her hand, its leather damp with sweat. Her flashlight flickered in her grip, and cast long, quivering shadows. The scent grew thicker the deeper she went, earth, iron, and old antiseptic.

The beam caught on something, a thin, vertical crack in the far wall. She stepped closer. The wall felt warm, as if something lived inside it.

She pressed her hand flat against the stone. A deep shudder passed through the foundation, like the house was bracing itself. Then, the wall gave way with a low moan. It split open to reveal a narrow passage carved into the stone. The air inside was colder. But it pulsed faintly, like breath moving through buried lungs. She stepped through.

The hidden chamber was circular. The stone walls bore scorch marks and faint carvings, half-erased by time. Shelves lined the edges, bowed under the weight of jars, boxes, and rusted tools. A thick stench of mildew and copper hung in the air.

In the center of the room sat an ancient wooden table. Deep gouges and burn marks covered its surface. In the center, a complex sigil had been carved, all sharp lines and spirals, pulsing faintly like a heartbeat. She didn't know what the words meant but they were clear.

She reached out. Her fingertips grazed the grooves. Then, the temperature plummeted. The shadows pulled together, forming a shape in the center of the room. It rose tall, too tall, and held no clear face. Just a suggestion of limbs, a hollow mass that flickered like candlelight. That was the violent thing in the attic. She swallowed.

"You shouldn't be here," it said. Its voice a rasp of nails and steel.

Her knees trembled. Her breath fogged in the cold air. "You've taken enough," she said, barely above a whisper. "You can't have me too."

The shape stepped forward. The floor moaned beneath it. "You are already mine."

The diary nearly fell from her shaking hands, but she forced herself to flip to the final page. The one Alura Hayes had written with a shaking hand, words etched like claw marks.

She slammed the book down on the table. The sigil flared bright, blinding for a second. Gabriella placed her hands over it and shouted the words scribbled in the margins, a chant, a ward, a plea. She followed it with the words around the sigil. She didn't know if she were banishing the entity... or calling a greater evil. She had to do something.

The room screamed. The walls vibrated. The shelves toppled. Jars shattered. Black sludge hissed across the stone floor. The shadow figure twisted violently, its form warping, arms splitting into writhing strands.

"No! You don't belong here!" it howled.

She screamed back, voice cracking. "Neither do you!"

The figure lunged, and then disintegrated, shredded like smoke by wind. The silence that followed was pure. Total.

She collapsed to her knees; her hands still pressed against the diary. Her body trembling from head to toe. The sigil faded to black. The air settled. When she climbed the stairs again, the house felt different.

The air no longer pushed against her skin. The shadows no longer whispered. Outside, the world looked brighter. Not just sunlight, but clarity. She stepped onto the porch and felt warmth on her face. She wanted to believe it was over.

But as she turned to look back, the house seemed to shimmer, just slightly. Its windows held a flicker of something waiting. Inside her chest, beneath the fading rush of adrenaline, something else stirred. The thing was gone. But the house was not finished.

Chapter 38

Aubrey came home three days later. She knew the moment the front door opened. Not because of the sound, though the latch clicked too softly, too carefully, but because the house changed. The air tightened. It became hauntingly familiar. The temperature dropped a degree, maybe two. The quiet that followed was not the house settling. It was the house listening.

She stayed where she was, seated at the dining table, hands folded around a coffee mug gone cold. The evening light slanted in through the windows, dust motes hung motionless, as if they, too, held their breath.

Footsteps crossed the entryway. Slow. Unhurried. "Gabriella," Aubrey called. His voice sounded wrong. Not angry. Not tired. Almost... light.

She stood, careful to keep the table between them as he entered the room. He looked the same at first glance, same coat, same posture, but there was a stillness to him that hadn't been there before. Like something inside him had finally stopped pretending.

"You're home early," she said.

"I missed you," he replied, smiling. The smile didn't reach his eyes. It was a lie. She didn't know why he said it.

Her pulse quickened, but her voice stayed even. "You didn't text."

"I thought I'd surprise you."

The house creaked overhead. Not a warning. A recognition. She didn't ask where he'd been. She didn't ask why he smelled faintly metallic, sharp and medicinal beneath his cologne. She didn't step closer.

"I want you to know something," she said instead. "Before you say whatever it is you came here to say."

His head tilted, curious. Amused.

"You will never put me in a hospital," she said. "Not anywhere. No matter how hard you try to convince people I'm insane. No matter how crazy you think you can make me look."

For a moment, he stared at her. Then he laughed. It startled her, not loud, not cruel, just genuine. A short, surprised sound, like she'd misunderstood the entire game.

"A hospital?" he said. "Gabriella... I never even considered that." Her stomach dropped. He reached into his coat pocket.

She moved back instinctively, but he was already holding it... a syringe, filled, the barrel catching the light. Clear liquid. No label.

"It was never about hospitalizing you," he said calmly. He stepped closer. "I was always going to kill you."

The words landed with terrifying simplicity. "You weren't supposed to last this long..." he continued. "You have enough Eidophrene in your body right now to poison a town. But you adapted, somehow, your body won't accept it. Your tolerance makes things... complicated. The divorce complicates things even more, but it's nothing I can't handle."

She lunged for the chair and swung it between them. The syringe slipped from his fingers as he dodged. It skidded across the hardwood floor, spinning, before coming to rest near the hall.

They froze. Then they ran. They hit the floor hard, bodies colliding, the impact driving the air from her lungs. His weight crushed down on her, stronger than she remembered, stronger than he should have been. His hand closed around her wrist, forcing it down. His knee pinned her thigh.

"You don't understand what you're part of," he hissed.

"I understand enough," she gasped, and slammed her forehead into his nose.

194

He roared, reeling back. Blood spilled hot across her face. She rolled, scrambling, toward the syringe. He grabbed her ankle and yanked her back. Her fingers brushed plastic. Missed.

They fought like animals, scratching, choking, slipping on overturned furniture. It was surreal. She kept thinking of the man she thought she married. But this wasn't him. She had to keep reminding herself. She would never raise her hands to him, just as he would never raise his hands to her. But that was gone. The house groaned around them, walls shuddering, something deep in the structure responding to the violence.

She saw it then, the syringe inches from her hand. She reached like her life depended on it. Her fingers closed around it just as his hand wrapped around her throat. Stars burst behind her eyes.

She didn't hesitate. She drove the needle into his thigh and slammed the plunger down.

He screamed. Not in pain, in shock. "No," he rasped. "That wasn't...."

His body violently convulsed. He collapsed, limbs jerking, eyes wide and unseeing. The smell of ozone filled the room. Something burned, sharp and electrical. Then... silence.

She crawled backward, gasping, watching him lie still. Dead. Relief surged through her so fast it made her dizzy.

Then the house screamed.

His body arched violently. His spine bent at an impossible angle, mouth opening wide as blackness poured into it, not smoke, not shadow, but something else. His eyes snapped open, glowing wrong, voice tearing free of him like something breaking through glass.

"She is mine." The thing wearing him stood. She stumbled back, blood slick on her hands. Her heart hammering so hard it hurt.

"No," she whispered.

The air split. Allura appeared first, her form pale but solid, eyes blazing with fury. Charlie followed, smaller but fierce, clutching her hand.

"You don't get him," Allura said. The thing laughed through Aubrey's mouth. Then it lunged.

The spirits hit it at once. Allura screamed words ripped from grief and rage, Charlie clinging, pulling, tearing. The house shook violently. Walls cracked. Lights exploded. The floor split beneath them.

Father roared, a sound that bent reality, clawing at Aubrey's body, trying to keep its hold. Allura wrapped herself around him. "Let go," she said. "It's over."

Charlie screamed. The three forms collapsed inward, light, shadow, fury, until there was a blinding flash and then nothing.

Silence. Aubrey's body hit the floor hard. It did not move again. She sat amid the wreckage, chest heaving, ears ringing, surrounded by splintered wood and broken glass. The house was quiet. Not watchful. Not hungry. Just empty. Just tired.

She stayed in the same spot. She just stared at his body, at the place where something ancient and cruel had finally lost its grip. She cried softly. Quietly. For a man who never existed.

Chapter 39

The air still trembled with what had been hours before. The residual echo of something vast and terrible being pulled apart. The remnants of Father, that roiling, ancient presence, had been dragged into whatever hell the house had once been a veil for. The room smelled faintly of scorched dust and old metal, as if lightning had struck somewhere close.

Even now, she couldn't move any more. Couldn't breathe properly. Her limbs felt heavy, jelly-like. A slick coldness clung to her neck and chest, the kind that came not from sweat but from the draining of everything human inside her. The world tilted at the edges, shadows smearing across her vision like wet ink.

Then... a knock. A voice. "Gabriella?"

James.

She tried to answer, but her throat locked. Her lips parted, but the sound came out dry, empty, like air through cracked glass. The front door banged open. His footsteps raced across the warped floorboards, rapid, uneven, shaking the house from its long, stunned stillness.

"Oh my god," he breathed. "Gabriella!"

His hands gripped her shoulders, firm and steady. His touch was warm, too warm, a shock against her clammy skin. The moment he touched her, the edges of the world returned. The colors sharpened. The floor steadied beneath her. She checked her neck for a pulse.

"I think I'm okay." She managed, though her voice was hardly more than a whisper.

His gaze followed hers to the body on the floor. The room shifted around them. His expression froze. Shock first. Then horror. And finally, the steady, grounded weight of resolve.

"We need to alert the authorities." He said, already dialing on his phone.

The air was thin, metallic, laced. It smelled like the moment after a storm: when something has broken, but not everything has settled.

Within another hour, red and blue lights began to bleed through the windows. They flashed across the walls in rhythmic pulses, and washed the house in waves of color, crimson, cobalt, white. Voices echoed through the hallways: sharp, clipped, professional. Boots scuffed against the floorboards. Gloves snapped into place.

The scent of latex and disinfectant filled the air. The house, once full of whispers, was now an open wound under examination. The ambulance was coming to check her out.

James stayed close. His presence a steady anchor. He didn't say much, only kept a hand resting lightly on hers. His thumb traced small, steady circles against her skin, grounding her against the hum of police radios and the scrape of evidence boxes being packed.

The EMTs checked her out, but nothing was broken. They could already see she would have extensive sprains and bruising, but nothing that warranted the emergency room. Later, one of the forensic techs called from the basement.

"Found something," he said, voice echoing off the cement.

They descended together. The basement smelled damp, the earthy scent of stone and rust, mixed with something faintly chemical. The flashlight beams cut through the dark in the corner. The light bounced off metal and dust.

A tech knelt beside the water softener. Its surface filmed with grime and corrosion. He flicked on a smaller light and leaned close. "It's a standard water softener," he murmured. "But look here."

Her pulse skipped.

The tech reached beneath the main casing and drew out a small device attached to the intake pipe. No larger than a pack of cigarettes, sleek and pale, a faint blue pulse beating from its core like a living thing. Its surface bore a familiar symbol, the faint, faded insignia of Aubrey's lab.

"Looks like a microdispersion module," the tech said. His voice was calm but distant, as if he already understood the weight of what he'd found. "Used to distribute measured doses into water lines. Controlled release. But this isn't standard. Someone's modified it."

Her stomach twisted. The air seemed to tilt again and pressed in close. So, the lab really didn't work on appliances. That made much more sense.

"What does it do?" James asked quietly.

The tech hesitated, pulling on a pair of gloves that snapped against his wrists. "Depends on the compound. But based on the residue... my guess? You've been drinking it. Showering in it. Breathing it in through steam... for months."

The hum of the fluorescent light above them seemed to grow louder. She took a single, trembling breath. "It was him," she whispered. "All of it... the hallucinations, the dreams, the gaps in memory. He was dosing me the entire time."

James's jaw clenched so tightly that his cheek twitched. The tech nodded grimly. "We'll test it, but... this wasn't accidental exposure. Someone monitored this. Doses, intervals, effects. It's all too precise. Like you were... the subject of an experiment."

She closed her eyes. Her pulse thundered in her ears. She already knew what they would find.

Project EIDOLON.

The name whispered through her thoughts like a toxin. All those months of doubting herself, of questioning her sanity, of feeling the walls of reality close in, it had been built, measured, administered. She had been engineered to break.

The officers then found a series of cameras set up through the house. She was being monitored and watched, and she didn't even know it. It shouldn't surprise her as much as it did. She quietly wept as they pulled cameras from every space.

She thought of the locket, still warm from her grasp. Of Allura's diary, the trembling script, the warnings. Of Charlie's soft, terrified voice: *He's just like Father.* It had happened before. And it had almost happened again.

James touched her arm gently. His thumb brushed over the bruise that formed there. "You're safe now," he said. "Whatever this was... it's over."

She didn't answer right away. Her gaze drifted upward, to the ceiling beams dark with age, to the shadows pooled in the corners that no longer moved.

"Maybe," she whispered finally

Chapter 40

The house had grown unnaturally quiet. Not the gentle quiet of morning, but the kind that pressed against the eardrums, heavy and absolute. She knew it was over, but it felt like a vacuum had been left in its wake.

She sat on the edge of the bed. Her bare feet rested on the cool wooden floor. Her fingers traced the worn leather of Allura's diary. The air smelled faintly of dust and rain seeping in from the eaves. She heard the faint hum of the refrigerator downstairs, the occasional tick of the radiator, mundane sounds that somehow made the silence feel louder.

The subsequent investigation dragged on for months. James had burst in through the door that day, his voice raw with panic. Authorities followed. Cameras. Statements. Evidence. She had been a test subject.

They had only recently finished deconstructing Aubrey's materials. The Eidophrene devices were removed and taken by the police first. Technicians flushed every pipe in the house to ensure the substance was gone. She had to rewash all her clothes and everything in the kitchen. Aubrey left a schematic of the surveillance apparatus in the office, so the authorities had a blueprint to remove everything he used to watch her.

The pages of Allura's diary were soft at the edges now, their corners darkened by oils from her fingertips. She had read the same passages so many times that she could recite them in her sleep. The last, desperate words of a woman who had lived and died in the same house, writing by candlelight as the darkness pressed in. The ink faded near the end, her words slanting into near illegibility.

They tell me I am ill. But I know the truth. The house keeps the memory of what it consumes.

She traced that final line with her fingertip. The air in the room felt charged, as though the house recognized its own name. Somewhere in the walls, something shifted, just enough to be noticed, just enough to make her hold her breath.

Aubrey was gone. Sometimes she caught herself saying it aloud, just to test the words in the air. *He's gone.* They always sounded too light, too fragile, to hold the weight of what he had done.

His death had been sudden and vicious, yet strangely quiet in its final moment. One moment, he had been a force dead set on killing her, shouting, his voice slicing like broken glass. The next, he was clutching his chest, his breath rattling, his body collapsing in on itself.

She could still hear the thud when he hit the floor. Still smell the faint trace of iron and ozone that lingered afterward. The memory played on loop, visceral, looping through her mind with a clarity that refused to fade.

The coroner had written cardiac arrest in tidy block letters. That was what people preferred, neat endings, medical explanations, words that closed doors instead of opening them. But she saw the other truth in the way his skin paled. In the brief shimmer of something black beneath his veins. Whatever he had created had devoured him from the inside out.

She hadn't cried. Not since. What she remembered most clearly wasn't horror but relief. As if the air itself had expanded, as if some invisible pressure inside the house had finally eased its grip. And yet the relief felt traitorous, tangled with guilt that pulsed beneath every quiet breath she took.

The days that followed blurred together, heavy with the slow drag of exhaustion. She tried to pack away his things, but every drawer she opened smelled faintly of him, aftershave, paper, chemicals. She donated his suits, his watches, his lab equipment, each object feeling like a confession she couldn't fully read.

Sometimes she would stop mid-motion and sense something in the air behind her. A faint shift. A breath. Once, while boxing up his books, she thought she heard his voice, soft, almost amused. *"You'll never really leave me."*

The words were so clear she dropped the book she was holding. It hit the floor spine-first, pages splaying open to a section on chemical neurology. She didn't pick it up for a long time.

The next morning, sunlight spilled across the walls, catching the motes of dust that danced like drifting ash. For once, it didn't look like decay. It looked like something suspended, alive but still.

She cleaned. She scrubbed the baseboards, polished the banister until the wood gleamed. She threw open the windows and let the wind rush in, carrying the smell of rain and the faint tang of iron from the garden.

Outside, the flowerbeds had grown wild, tangled with weeds and stubborn roots. The soil was damp and cold under her gloves as she dug in, pulling and pruning, turning over the earth until it breathed again. She unearthed old toys, a spoon, bits of rusted metal, a past that hadn't entirely let go.

Every handful of dirt left a shadow beneath her nails, and yet, she didn't mind. The ache in her hands was real, tangible. The earth grounded her. In the distance, crows gathered on the edge of the trees, silent and still. Watching. But they didn't move closer.

As the sun dipped low, she sat on the porch with a cup of tea, her palms sore and raw. The smell of fresh-turned soil lingered in the air, mingled with the faint sweetness of jasmine that had somehow survived neglect. A wind chime tinkled once and then went still.

The house behind her stood silent, its windows catching the dying light. From this angle, they looked almost kind, reflecting the orange of the sunset, softening the sharp edges that had once seemed so cruel.

For the first time, she felt something close to peace. Not freedom. Not yet. But peace.

She watched as twilight gathered, the horizon fading into deep blue. The first star blinked faintly overhead. Her breath came steady and unhurried.

Then, just at the edge of hearing, something shifted. A single creak from within the house. So soft it might have been settling wood. Or footsteps. The kind of sound that made the body go still before the mind could reason with it.

She didn't turn around. It really was just the house settling. She stared into the garden instead, at the dark soil she'd unearthed, the faint shimmer of new frost catching moonlight.

Her heartbeat steadied. Whatever lived in the house could stay there. Whatever lived in her, she could carry.

For now, that was enough. A cool wind swept through the yard, lifting a few stray pages from Allura's diary where they rested on the porch rail. The paper fluttered once, twice, then slid gently to the ground.

The house behind her exhaled, a deep, almost imperceptible sigh. She closed her eyes. And the night swallowed the sound.

Chapter 41

The sun broke over the ridge casting long amber fingers through the lace curtains. Dust danced in the golden light, swirling slowly in the quiet air of the house. The lingering shadows and strange sounds in her home were all but gone. She'd came to believe the sounds were part of the home's age, but evidently they weren't.

She stood barefoot in the living room. Her skin chilled from the cold floorboards beneath her. The room smelled faintly of dried roses and wood polish, with a whisper of something older beneath it, like forgotten earth and burnt paper. The silence was real now. Not oppressive. Not watchful. Just... silence.

Allura appeared in the archway first. Her presence was softer than ever. Her form shimmered faintly, like morning mist that caught firelight. Her eyes, deep pools of sorrow and strength, were fixed on Gabriella.

"It's time," she said gently. Her voice carried the sound of distant rain, a rhythm that had once lulled a child to sleep. Charlie stood beside her, hands clasped. His eyes were wide, hopeful, but tinged with the deep ache of parting.

"Are you free?"

Allura nodded. "He can't hold us anymore."

Charlie stepped forward and wrapped his arms around Gabriella's waist. His body passed through her slightly, cool and light, like wind brushing across skin. But the warmth of the gesture filled her chest.

"I wish I could've helped you more," he whispered.

"You did more than anyone," she said, her voice cracked. "You saved me. Both of you did."

Allura stepped forward, her hand brushed Gabriella's shoulder like the flutter of silk. "You were the one who was brave enough to face him. Both of them. That was never our burden to carry."

"I'll miss you," she whispered.

Charlie smiled, his face glowing faintly. "We won't be far." With a soft shimmer, like the breeze brushing wind chimes, they were gone. The silence that followed was warm. Clean. She closed her eyes and basked in it.

The light outside deepened. It turned from gold to pink to violet. She watched as their outlines thinned and became something lighter. Something brighter.

That was the end of the dead in her home... that she knew of. The authorities collected all the remains from the attic two weeks earlier. They took the ancient medical records to see if they could identify any of them. The records would then be sent to the local historical society for archiving. In total, 43 people, or parts of them, were interred in that chamber.

Dr. Reyland Hayes received the same treatment as Aubrey. He genuinely had some fame locally. Many believed he tried his best to cure influenza. The reality of his research practices was exposed along with the medical documents. He received much of the same blowback Aubrey had.

He married his nurse soon after Allura and Charlie died. No one questioned why she met the same fate they did the next year. The year after that, he died in a lab explosion. The family tried to live in the estate for years before deciding to sell it.

The mysterious packages were from Michael Andrews. Leigh's husband. They met several times for coffee to trade war stories. It helped. He was a researcher at the lab in a different department.

He just started out trying to get a divorce for neglect and infidelity. He gathered evidence on Leigh, and Aubrey, for over a year. He was going to divorce Leigh and take custody of their three children.

He never imagined to stumble upon what he did. Once he found the width and depth of the unethical and illegal activities, he stopped just worrying about divorce and began amassing evidence for the authorities.

He quietly looked for work at laboratories elsewhere. He knew the Bainbridge Institute would shut down once the authorities were involved. He was already speaking with agents from Virginia's Bureau of Criminal Investigation when Aubrey tried to kill her. An investigation of that magnitude would close the facility indefinitely, maybe a year, maybe permanently.

Once everything came to light, Michael had paternity tests on all three kids. Two belonged to Aubrey but called him dad. He had no plans to tell any of them they weren't his.

She eventually met them. It made her heart hurt, but she wouldn't tell him. They looked like their biological father. They were beautiful. They should've been her children.

The most damning evidence at the Banbridge Institute was from Aubrey himself, buried in files encrypted but not irretrievable. Doses calibrated over time. Cognitive markers logged. Emotional thresholds tested. Her entire descent into madness had been orchestrated. Measured. Cataloged. It seemed particularly chilling to the rest of the world that someone would treat their spouse like an expendable lab rat.

Aubrey had sensors installed in her rings that tracked her pulse, oxygen, and blood pressure. He was affectionate when they first moved in to get everything in place without raising suspicion.

He frequently drugged her at night when they moved into the house. She was a light sleeper, and he dosed her with sedatives. That was the purpose of always getting her food and bringing it home or bringing her a glass of wine. He'd conducted EEGs and even blood tests while she slept. She overslept when the contractors arrived that first day, because she'd been sedated. She felt that bizarre flu so often, particularly so when he had sedated her.

Aubrey installed the cameras after the renovations, when he was confident no workmen would find them. He could come to the house whenever he felt like it. He had house keys. She never thought to ask for them back. She inadvertently gave him access to turn the whole house into an observatory. He didn't get involved in the renovation because that was never the real purpose.

She was still mortified. She'd started seeing a therapist, who told her that her response was natural, but knowing it was 'natural' didn't alleviate it. It simply let her express her humiliation.

She felt like such a fool. A ridiculous and naïve fool. She was certain the rest of the world felt the same, most were just too polite to say anything. She wanted to be a *survivor.* To be seen as strong and capable. If only she could convince herself. She didn't know if she could ever trust anyone again. Even Michael and James. They were the closest things she had to friends, but the damage was just done.

She also discovered Aubrey's condo near the lab. That was his real home. It was entirely cold and white minimalist. That was him. It was the hardest place to visit. She wandered through it in disbelief. She had never visited a place that felt so hateful.

Even through stark utility, there were indications of the life she wanted, of the life he denied. He had family photographs on the walls that resembled those on his desk. She felt his presence there. He had a closet full of clothes, so his trips back the house were nothing more than to check on his experiment. She cried there. She could still hear him, *"You're overwrought again, Gabriella."* Yes, she was.

She packed up his personal items and took them home. She donated his clothing and accessories, just as she had with the things at her house. Even his toiletries. She put the condo up for sale that day. Michael didn't want his children seeing any of Aubrey's things.

She sat by the firepit in the backyard every evening, burning a little more of that life away. She hoped beyond hope Aubrey could see everything he cherished go up in flames. The only thing that could possibly equal her embarrassment was her loathing of him.

She read his phone's messages, emails on his laptop, and all the while, wondered who he really was. He was a wholly different person. It went far beyond infidelity or their marital issues. Simple pleasures he said he hated, he'd really loved. Things he always seemed to enjoy with her, were all things he hated. Those whom he said were friends, actually barely knew him. It was all so pointless. He lied about everything, for no reason at all. Maybe it was to keep her distant. To ensure she really knew nothing about him. Maybe he'd been planning this experiment for years.

Leigh, along with three other researchers, were indicted for a plethora of felonies. Though the lab denied involvement, leaked emails confirmed they'd known. They had monitored everything. The three were charged with attempted first-degree murder at the forefront. She really was never supposed to survive. Eidophrene is undetectable unless a coroner tests for it and it is fatal in large doses. No one could say why she wasn't dead, too.

Aubrey's accreditations were revoked posthumously. His siblings were all wealthy and powerful in their own right. All lived in much larger cities and had established lives there. They attended Francis's services but left right after. None attended Aubrey's.

His estate, vast, secretive, powerful, was transferred entirely to her. A twisted reward for surviving what he considered his life's work. She didn't want it. But the law didn't ask. The Bainbridge name now sat on her deed, her bank accounts, her mail. She sold the main Bainbridge estate but kept Murkwood.

She moved slowly in those weeks. Her limbs often felt too heavy, her thoughts distant. Simple tasks, boiling water, folding laundry, locking the front door, took effort. The doctor said Eidophrene might take months to flush out of her body. Or years. There was also the possibility it would never truly be gone. The substance was too new and had no documented history.

She wasn't accustomed to her new celebrity status. She had to fix the gate and fence to keep the media out. Who knew one unremarkable woman could inadvertently cause such repercussions? She'd been interviewed, studied, and there was talk of a book deal. She didn't want to be the center of attention. She'd just wanted a nice, simple, predictable life.

New laws were before congress to ensure nothing like that could occur again. The Bainbridge Institute was enshrouded in scandal, and the authorities froze their assets and projects. The governmental agencies working with the lab had withdrawn all interests.

She tried to find the mysterious basement room again. The charred room that was clearly a place of ritual. All that was left was a barren pantry with a few empty shelves.

James continued to regularly visit. He didn't hover. He didn't demand. He sat with her on the porch at dusk, the mug of coffee always between his hands. The smell of cinnamon and cedar often lingering around him. She spoke little. He asked little. But his presence was solid, a human tether to something real.

Sometimes, in the deepest part of the night, she would wake and listen. No footsteps. No whispers. No breath that wasn't her own. The house was just a house now. It creaked in the wind; it sighed when it settled. It held the heat unevenly. But it no longer pulsed with that strange, hungry awareness.

Still, she didn't sleep easily. She worked the garden every morning. She turned the soil, pulled weeds, and planted fresh bulbs. The earth was wet and cool between her fingers. She let it coat her hands, get into her cuticles, ground her.

James built her a bench by the jasmine vines. The wood was pale and smooth. She sat there every afternoon. Sometimes she thought of Aubrey. Sometimes she thought of Charlie.

But mostly, she thought about what it meant to keep going. To rebuild something inside her that had been broken for so long she didn't even know what it meant to be whole. She was still numb. But she was also still here.

And somewhere deep beneath the ache, something was beginning to grow. Not hope. Not yet. But roots. And maybe, in time, that would be enough.

About the Author

L. Chambers Wright, who also publishes as Laura Wright, is a lifelong storyteller, researcher, and writer of fiction that treads the blurred lines between memory and myth. From her home in the Appalachian foothills, she writes surrounded by books, rescued typewriters, and a handful of keys that don't seem to belong anywhere. Her work is rooted in place, language, and the strange traces people leave behind. More at laurawrites.net.

Other Books by L. Chambers Wright

Virginia Creeper
Infectious
The Moon Sees Me
Hangar 408
Beneath the Wych Elm
Monarch
The Demon Machine
Witchbook
Black Diamond
The Longest Night
Six Days
Death's Head Rose

As Laura Wright

Bizarre Tri-Cities
Haunted Appalachia
The History of Bad Men (series)
Appalachian Curiosities
Shivers: Folklore and Ghost Stories Retold by Laura Wright

Secrets of the Melungeons
The Girl In the Trees